Dying
to
Cruise

Dawn Brookes

Dying
to
Cruise

A Rachel Prince Mystery

Dawn Brookes

Oakwood Publishing

Paperback Edition 2019
Kindle Edition 2019
Paperback ISBN: 978-1-913065-00-3
Copyright © DAWN BROOKES 2019
Cover Design: Janet Dado

Dedicated to Prince

Chapter 1

Florence Flanders hurriedly packed a final few belongings in her suitcase, and then closed the laptop she'd been staring at for the past twenty minutes. This message was more threatening and considerably more toxic than the others she had been receiving over the past six months.

The first email had arrived towards the end of autumn the previous year. She remembered it clearly because it was around the same time as she had got in touch with the love of her life, the one that got away. Now she would be seeing him again, for the first time in over sixty years, and despite her eighty-one years, the same fluttering in her stomach, a reminder of times gone by, appeared each time she imagined their reunion.

As Florence placed the laptop in her briefcase, she thought about each spiteful message that had come from an unknown 'do not reply' email address. This in itself suggested the person was able to send it from an encrypted server. Initially she had laughed, thinking the first email was some sort of prank or payback from a disgruntled former employee. There had been plenty of those during her long career, some of whom had threatened to do her harm, but when push came to shove they were just wimps. She believed she had always been a fair if somewhat formidable boss, but one had to be as a woman in business in those days; even now she had read somewhere that women had to work twice as hard to be considered half as good as men at the top. There were so many sharks in the business world and Australia hadn't quite rid itself of macho types or stereotypical behaviours. Florence did not tolerate either sharks or shirkers.

The poison pen letters in the form of emails had become more frequent and more threatening as each month passed. To begin with they were just nasty and personal, but now they were darker and sicker, describing in detail how the person signing off as Z was going to enjoy killing her for sins of the past. Florence was nearing the day she would work out who Z was as the emails had become clumsy, referring to past events she remembered, and she realised with horror it was someone she once knew.

When she told her old lover about the threats and how sinister they were, he agreed to meet her for the Bucket List Cruise: a cruise she had invented to coax people with money to take the trip of a lifetime before they shifted off this mortal coil. It was convenient that the emails had become more menacing, but she would have enticed him one way or another, and although she really was beginning to fear the psycho sending the messages meant business, it was a price worth paying for the meeting with the man whom she had never stopped loving. But the hard truth of who might be sending the emails was too horrendous to contemplate.

Her son, Joe, had been livid when she'd told him she was coming along for the tour.

"Why can't you just let me manage the business, Mother? You said you were going to start taking a back seat and let me get on with things. You're not getting any younger, you know."

Florence had viewed her son, fifty-seven years old, weak and yet pugnacious, and still trying to wrestle his way to the top. "I've changed my mind, I will be coming whether you like it or not. Anyway, I might enjoy myself. It's been a while since I went on a cruise. I won't interfere."

"You will, Mother, you always do. Please don't come, I just want to be able to spend some time with my family." His pleading baby-blue eyes would usually have done the trick, but not this time.

Stupid man! His comments were a red rag to a bull. She snarled at him, barely able to keep her temper. "I AM FAMILY, more so than that bimbo you've married. It's time you took a look in the mirror, Joseph." She knew how much he hated being called Joseph. "You're ruining your life, and the life of your daughter. She hardly ever sees her mother. You have no idea about running your 'so-called' family, let alone a business. Now get out and leave me alone."

He did leave, slamming the door behind him, and obviously went straight to the 'new model', more generous in bosom than in nature, but Florence didn't underestimate the rival for her son's affections. The younger woman, almost half her son's age, was astute and already managing to fleece him of the Trust Fund left to him by his late father. Florence wouldn't put it past her to be the sender of the emails, but didn't think she'd have the imagination or the guts. Besides, if she was right and it was someone from her past, Chloe Flanders didn't fit the profile. She would stay on the list for now, though.

It was hard to narrow it right down, but Florence was certain both the malicious poison email writer and her old flame would be aboard the *Coral Queen*. She would need to have her wits about her and be on high alert.

Chapter 2

Rachel passed through security, ignoring the knowing smiles and smirks on the faces of some of the crew that revealed her reputation as cruise ship sleuth had preceded her and spread more widely than she'd anticipated. Although this was only her fourth voyage, the murders on the previous three, and her involvement in solving them, had obviously gained her a certain notoriety.

A few familiar faces made her feel at home and the embarkation routine no longer filled her with awe. She could even spot new cruisers boarding the ship as they gazed around in wonder at the opulent surroundings in the main atrium.

The atrium was always a hive of activity and today was no exception, the area buzzing with energy as passengers arrived full of excitement and anticipation. Seasoned cruisers made straight for the welcome waiters carrying trays of champagne while first-timers held back, unsure whether the drinks were free or not.

Rachel watched and listened to accents from all around the world, occupying herself by guessing how many waiters she'd recognise while waiting for her room to be made ready. Children ran around excitedly, exploring the area that spanned two decks while their parents attempted to keep their own excitement under control.

"Rachel!" a familiar voice called from across the room.

She waved at the small Filipino man heading her way. Dressed in his pristine white officer's uniform, he embraced her.

"Hello, Bernard, how are you?"

"Excited to see you on board, things have been far too quiet around here." He leaned in and whispered, "No murders."

She thumped him gently on the arm. "Nor will there be this time, I'm determined. Where's Sarah?"

Sarah, Rachel's best friend since childhood, and Bernard were nurses aboard the *Coral Queen*.

"She's finishing up in the passenger lounge off-ship; she'll be here soon. I was ordered to keep a lookout for you. I'm not on duty for another few hours. Do you mind if I join you?"

"I'd be delighted," she answered, proffering the seat opposite with a nod of her head. "I'm really pleased to be here at last, but feel thoroughly jetlagged." Rachel had flown to Adelaide via Singapore from Heathrow the day before, before staying overnight in a local hotel paid for by Queen Cruises: all part of a compensation package from the previous cruise. This time she would even be paid for taking the cruise, being a guest speaker. She had passed through numerous time zones and wasn't quite sure, but thought she was a day ahead of when she'd left England.

"I'm not surprised you're jetlagged, those long-haul flights are killers. Not that you look any worse for wear – beautiful as ever. We came the long way round, obviously. Half-world cruises take their toll, but I'd still prefer to sail rather than fly."

Loud voices pulled their attention away from the amicable conversation. Rachel turned around to see a significant number of elderly people being ushered along by a buxom woman with henna dyed hair falling in long, thin strands around her shoulders. The woman also wore a most unusual looking combination of smudged purple lipstick with bright red eye shadow, neither of which went with the hair.

Bernard laughed. "Rachel, your mouth is open."

She realised she had been gawping at the woman, who had to be in her eighties, bustling around giving orders to anyone in the group who would listen. The rest of the crowd gathering around her wore t-shirts of various colours and sizes, emblazoned with the large letters DTC standing out boldly on their chests.

"Whoops, sorry, Bernard! That hair is mesmerising. What does DTC stand for?"

Bernard looked confused for a moment, then slapped his head. "Ah, I know who they are now. We were told they would be boarding – lots of medical problems," he whispered again, smirking.

"So?"

"They are part of a bucket list tour party who have never cruised before. As far as I remember from Graham's briefing this morning, they're aged between seventy-five and ninety-five. I think there are forty-three expected, if they all make it." He laughed again.

"Bernard, one day that sense of humour of yours is going to get you into hot water."

"Oh it already has, many times, Rachel, but I'm never going to be politically correct. I get away with it because I can fake cultural differences and pretend I don't understand the problem."

"You still haven't told me what DTC stands for."

"That's because I have no idea. Maybe it's their travel agent." He sat back in his chair and they both watched the mixed group as more and more of them gathered. Rachel observed as they congregated in small groups. They appeared to be multi-nationals, but she detected lots of British and some Australian accents. The eccentric looking woman was trying to organise them into some sort of order, but the majority weren't playing ball.

"I hope none of them kick-the-bucket on their bucket list cruise."

"You couldn't resist that, could you?" Rachel cackled good-naturedly; she had been thinking the same thing.

"Actually, they all look very healthy from where I'm sitting."

"That's good because I think some of them have booked in for your self-defence classes."

Rachel groaned, nervous at the mention of her cruise lecturer responsibilities. Surveying the group for a little longer as the last few members gathered together, she caught sight of Sarah walking alongside the stragglers while vigorously writing notes.

Sarah looked up from her notebook and spotted Rachel. Her eyes lit up and she beamed, but was arrested from joining her by the woman with the unusual hair who had originally caught Rachel's attention.

"Nurse!" she commanded. "I need to have a word with you." Giving Rachel an apologetic look, Sarah was manoeuvred away from the large group now assembled.

Rachel frowned, but then smiled cheekily at Bernard. "You're going to be busy if that woman has her way."

Now it was Bernard's turn to groan as he looked up.

It was good to be aboard the cruise ship she had grown so fond of, and the Australia and New Zealand tour promised to be the opportunity of a lifetime.

"You have to give it them, it's a great choice of destination for their bucket list."

Bernard smiled and the pair chatted freely, with Bernard filling Rachel in on the latest cruise ship gossip.

"Baby doc has been dating Greta, a German woman who works in Guest Services. Seems it's getting serious."

Alessandro Romano was the junior doctor on board the *Coral Queen*, known as Alex, or baby doc to the crew. Rachel had met him a few times, both informally and in his medical capacity following injuries sustained on previous cruises.

"I'm pleased, I hope it works out. Although from what I hear, romantic liaisons are all too common between crew on board cruise liners and don't tend to last."

"Not so much amongst officers. We have to behave ourselves."

Rachel raised an eyebrow, knowing full well that Bernard didn't know the meaning of the word behave. Although he was not unfaithful to his wife, he was a pleasant mischief maker.

"It seems all the medical team is hitched now apart from Graham, who says he'll never marry again, Brigitte and Gwen." Senior nurse Gwen Sumner had been burned by a relationship on her last ship. "Actually, that's only half the team, isn't it?" He counted the team members out on his fingers. "Can you believe I'm the only one that's married? Says a lot about cruise ship life. I don't think Gwen's ever been married."

Rachel knew about Gwen's affair with the chief medical officer from a previous ship, but she didn't know much about Dr Graham Bentley's background. Dr Bentley, who she couldn't bring herself to call Graham, was the chief medical officer, or CMO, and in charge of the medical team. Gwen, an Australian woman in her forties who Rachel had got to know and like, directly managed the nurses, and then there was Brigitte, a young French nurse around the same age as herself and Sarah.

"Why won't Dr Bentley marry again? Did he have a nasty divorce?"

"No, far from it, he doted on his wife who died of cancer. He doesn't talk about it, but I think that's why he continues working on board cruise ships. He hardly ever goes back to the marital home, but won't sell it either."

"That's sad, I didn't realise. Does he have children?"

"Four." Bernard laughed. "I thought my three were enough! In fact you might get to meet his two youngest: they are joining the cruise ship in Melbourne along with their wives and children."

"Are any of them doctors?"

"The youngest son is. He's a trauma surgeon, a chip off the old block I'm told – not that I really understand what that means. I think the other one is a dentist. He also has two daughters. The older is a lawyer, but I'm not sure about the other daughter. Graham doesn't mention her much, which suggests she might be the odd one out in the family."

"A chip off the old block means similar to his father," Rachel explained. "How's Waverley? He was engaged the last I heard. I suppose he's dreading me being on board?"

"Well he would be, but he's away on honeymoon. We have a temporary chief of security from the *Jade Queen* and I can tell you now, stay away from him. He's a very unpleasant man."

"Not that I have any intention of meeting him, but why do you say that?"

"I have a friend on board the *Jade*, and he says they are all putting the flags out. The deputy is in charge temporarily over there, and he's much nicer to work with."

"Why couldn't this ship's deputy take charge of the *Coral*? Not because she's a woman, I hope."

"No, although there are very few senior officers outside of catering and housekeeping that are women, so you may have picked something up there. Apparently she doesn't have enough experience which surprises me – Charlotte Franks is a very able senior officer. I haven't met the new guy yet, to be honest, so I should give him a fair hearing. I'm sure we'll get the lowdown from Sarah's boyfriend."

"What's that about my boyfriend?" Sarah appeared from behind Rachel and the two women shrieked and hugged each other. "Great to see you, Rachel."

"And you, I've missed you. You're blooming."

"Love is in the air," teased Bernard.

"Be quiet, you. And what were you saying about my boyfriend?"

"Rachel can explain. I have to go and eat before the safety drill. See you guys later." Bernard left the two women to catch up.

As the decibel level from the bucket list tour group was increasing, Sarah looked at Rachel. "Come on, let's find somewhere quiet."

At that moment, the announcement came over the ship's loud speakers informing passengers their rooms were ready.

"My room?" suggested Rachel. Sarah nodded.

Chapter 3

Rachel and Sarah found Rachel's stateroom on deck nine. She had been given a room with a balcony in return for lecturing on board the *Coral Queen*, and it was surprisingly large with a bathroom containing a tub as well as shower. There was a closet for hanging coats in the hallway and the living area consisted of a queen-sized bed with wall-mounted flat-screen TV, a large wardrobe with enough space for two, a sitting area with a bed-settee, two chairs, a table and a desk with mirrors. Tea and coffee making facilities were neatly laid out on the table.

A fully loaded fridge sat to one side of the desk and a small safe in the wardrobe was just about big enough for Rachel's laptop. A large pair of sliding doors led out to the balcony where there were two chairs and a table. The room was on the starboard side of the ship towards the bow.

"Not quite as luxurious as the suites on deck fifteen, but it will do," Rachel declared.

"I should say so. You're getting too spoilt." Sarah laughed. "Why didn't you opt for the suite?"

"The cruise line offered this room as part of the speaking engagement package along with free food. I used the compensation for flights and tours rather than waste it on a room. As well as the free food, I have drinks thrown in too." Rachel filled the kettle with fresh water and switched it on. "Tea?"

"Yes please, I'm parched. It feels like an age since breakfast."

"That's because it is, and well past lunchtime. Sarah Bradshaw, you need to take more care of yourself." Rachel caught movement out of the corner of her eye and realised the ship was leaving port. The announcement had probably been made, but the speakers were not yet switched on in her room, so she made a mental note to do this later.

The silent departures were always fascinating as the huge vessel moved away from the dockside with such grace. The only time Rachel was fully aware of setting sail was when on deck twelve where there was always a sailaway party and lively music hailing the ship's departure from each port.

She looked at her watch.

"Bang on time, as ever. Are you still on call?"

"No, Brigitte is on now until tomorrow morning, so unless there's an emergency, I only have to do evening surgery."

"Bernard was telling me about the bucket list group. Do you know what the DTC on their t-shirts stands for?"

"I didn't, but Mrs Flanders – the group leader, and a force to be reckoned with – informed me it stood for 'Dying to Cruise'. She guffawed when she told me; the t-shirts are a gimmick she came up with to encourage the group to gel with each other, and so that they could recognise who else was in their party."

"Don't tell me they have to wear those t-shirts all cruise?"

"I feared that too, but no, she informed me she has had badges made with the same lettering – branding, she called it – so they will have to wear those!" Sarah rolled her eyes and Rachel's eyebrows rose with amusement.

"Still, I think it's a great idea – not the DTC thing, but the bucket list cruise. I like the look of them – a feisty bunch, I imagine?"

"Not half! And if Mrs F – she told me to call her that, by the way – is anything to go by, they will be a demanding lot too. She gave me an ear-bashing about their dietary requirements, laundry needs, activity sessions," Sarah took an itinerary out of her pocket and waved it in the air, "and their touring demands. After regaling me with information, she scolded me for not taking notes."

"What's any of that got to do with you?"

"Absolutely zilch. But could I get her to understand that the medical team was only responsible for their health needs? Not at all."

Rachel laughed loudly as Sarah's exasperation surfaced. Being a cruise ship nurse was a challenging occupation at the best of times; although her friend loved the work, it did come with caveats.

"Poor Sarah, I'm sure Dr Bentley will put her right."

"I hope so, because if Mr Golding doesn't get his vegan meal and Mrs Chambers doesn't have her laundry seen to daily, I will be held personally responsible." Sarah mimicked the formidable Mrs F's voice, which made them both giggle hysterically. "I do hope the poor things are allowed to enjoy themselves because the ones I met with who actually *did* have medical problems seemed really nice."

"I'm sure they will have a great time. Your Mrs F – I assume she's the one with the henna dyed hair – can't be the official tour guide, surely?"

"No, apparently that's her son – Mr F, I can call him – her daughter-in-law and her son's daughter! I didn't meet them because they were in the purser's office helping those with expensive jewellery stash it away safely. You noticed her then? It all depends on whether they are able to get a word in edgeways with Mummy bossing them around. The son is fifty-seven, she informed me, and his wife is a new model – I don't think Mrs F approves. She's just turned thirty and his daughter's late twenties."

"Interesting dynamics, I wonder what the daughter thinks. Is there a Mr F senior?"

"I didn't like to ask in case it involved a long story or more dietary demands, and I haven't checked all their records yet. If I had asked, she's the type of woman who would accuse me of sexism or prying. I wasn't going to take that risk."

Rachel grinned as she handed Sarah her tea and took a seat next to her on the settee, placing her coffee down on the table. "It's so good to see you, Sarah, and you do look well."

"And you too, on both counts. I miss not having you around – the cruises haven't been as interesting without you."

"That's what Bernard said. Surely you of all people don't want another murder on board?"

"Certainly not! But I wouldn't mind a bit of a crime mystery, we've got used to them now."

Rachel liked the sparkle in her friend's deep brown eyes: she looked happy. "Nurse Bradshaw, I'm shocked. Is this Jason's influence?" Sarah had been dating one of the security guards, Jason Goodridge – an ex-army guy whom Rachel had met during her last cruise – for a few months.

"Not at all, he would prefer everything to go smoothly without mishap, particularly as Waverley's away for a month."

"I heard that. I'm disappointed, I was hoping to meet the woman who'd brought happiness into his life again."

"Now I think of it, we don't want any crimes on board at all, because the new man will not welcome your interference… hmm, help at all, from what I hear."

"Bernard told me that too. He sounds challenging, but you needn't worry about that. This time there will not be any murders."

"CODE BLUE DECK SIX LIBRARY. REPEAT, CODE BLUE DECK SIX!" Sarah's radio screeched to life and the girls locked on to each other's eyes briefly before she left the room hastily.

Chapter 4

Sarah was among the first of the medical team to arrive on the scene, along with Brigitte and Alex. A large crowd of passengers, mainly elderly, were blocking the way into the library.

"Excuse me please, medics," Sarah announced and a people-flanked corridor was immediately formed to allow them through, closing in again as soon as they'd passed.

Sarah recognised the large frame of Mrs Flanders immediately. The DTC initials were now smeared with blood, making the branded wear seem somewhat ironic. The elderly woman lay on the floor with long strands of hair forming a henna fan above her head like some sort of goddess from ancient mythology, but she was obviously no goddess and very much dead.

A frail elderly man wearing a pink turban and sporting a striking silver-grey beard and moustache stopped his attempt at resuscitation and turned towards them, shaking his head. The sweat-filled forehead suggested he wasn't used to the exercise and his fire-red face caused Sarah concern. Alex and Brigitte assessed the situation quickly, but the mauve appearance around the woman's lips, visible through the purple lipstick, along with the overall pallor and fixed-stare told them all they needed to know. As if that wasn't enough, the pool of blood congealing on the marble floor confirmed the hopelessness of any attempt at first aid. Alex checked the carotid for a pulse and shook his head, causing gasps and murmuring to filter through the ever-growing crowd.

Relieved to see security guards arriving, led by Jason, Sarah turned towards the elderly man while the security team cleared the area and went about rapidly erecting a cordon to seal off the grisly scene. Sarah handed him an antiseptic wipe to wash the small amount of blood from his hands and led him towards the rear of the library where she suggested he take a seat on one of the many reading chairs.

"I'll get you a drink. Any preference?"

"Brandy," he replied, his voice shaky.

Sarah stepped out of the library and caught one of the waiters. "Could you bring tea, water and a large brandy as quickly as possible?" she asked.

"On the way, Nurse." He spun around and headed towards the Plato Lounge Café.

Sarah was almost knocked over by the new chief of security, who marched into the library and briskly took command.

"What are these people doing here?" he snapped.

"They're potential witnesses, sir," Sarah heard Jason reply as she returned to her charge.

No sooner had she sat in the chair next to the man than the drinks arrived. She saw in the distance that Graham and Bernard had now joined the medics, and the crowd of officers were talking around the body.

"I'm Sarah Bradshaw, sir, an officer and nurse on board the ship," Sarah said, handing the large glass of brandy to the man. She was thankful his colour had returned to normal and he mopped his brow with a handkerchief. His long, thin fingers grasped the brandy and he took a sip.

"Manandeep Janda."

"Mr Janda, are you with the same tour party as the unfortunate lady?" His white jacket was buttoned up, presumably to hide the ridiculous t-shirt that lay beneath.

"I am a part of the bucket list tour, yes." He took a gulp of his brandy this time.

"Did you see what happened?"

"No, I had arranged to meet Florence in the library. We were going to choose a book for a book club event. When I arrived she was sitting on a chair with blood covering her chest; a knife lay on the floor." He mopped his brow again.

Sarah quizzed, "Sitting in a chair?"

"Yes. I'm sorry, I shouted for help and dragged her on to the floor to try to stem the bleeding and allow circulation to her heart and brain – I used to be a doctor, you see. Anyway, it was too late for any of that. I did what I could, but she was already dead." He gestured with his hands as if to emphasise how hopeless his attempt had been.

"I'll take over now, Nurse, thank you." A deep and gruff voice made the presence of the security chief known.

"I'm sorry for your shock, Mr Janda. If there's anything you need, please drop in to one of the surgeries we hold morning and evening, or request a stateroom visit." Sarah patted the man's hand before moving away and leaving the brusque chief of security to question him further.

"Janda, was it?" she heard him snap and felt sorry for the man, who had already been traumatised and would likely now undergo an interview akin to an interrogation, if her fleeting assessment of the CSO was anything to go by.

The cumbersome body of Mrs Flanders was being hoisted from the floor to a trolley stretcher by four security guards assisted by the medics. A sheet had been placed underneath the body to give them the leverage required to lift the deadweight on to the waiting stretcher.

"One, two, three, go." Graham took charge.

With a few grunts, the lift was a success and the sides were raised on the stretcher, although there was some bulging through the gaps. The body was covered with a clean sheet.

As they were leaving, Jason whispered to Sarah, "No-one else saw what happened, the Sikh guy was the first on scene. The rest of the witnesses came afterwards and didn't know what to do."

"The murderer saw what happened. This can't be happening, Jason," said Sarah grimly. "I'll catch you later."

"We'll find whoever did it, Sarah." He squeezed her hand.

"It's not that – it's just typical that Rachel happens to be on board again, and there's a murder. How will I keep her out of it?"

"You won't have to. He will." Jason nodded his head towards the formidable chief of security, who was still quizzing poor Mr Janda while barking out orders.

"Goodridge, in your own time!" yelled the chief.

Sarah huffed.

"The master calls, speak later." Jason shrugged his shoulders, smiled meekly and turned away.

After ensuring that all passengers were diverted away from the scene, the medical team wheeled the stretcher towards a service lift and transported it down to the morgue adjacent to the medical centre. Sarah followed.

Chapter 5

Rachel couldn't resist mingling with the crowds that had gathered outside of the library on deck six.

"Who was it?" She detected a Welsh lilt coming from a short sparrow-like woman with a pinched nose and silver-grey hair tied neatly into a bun on top of her head.

"That bossy woman who thought she was in charge," a tall, lean man with white hair, sideburns and a moustache answered. Ex-military, Rachel surmised. "Flanders or Mrs F as she liked to be called."

Another woman joined in the conversation. "Yes, it's definitely Mrs Flanders. Deep found her and tried to give her first aid."

"Is she…?"

"Dead? Yes, as dead as a dodo."

The short woman paled and swooned, and Rachel managed to catch her before she slid to the floor. She glared at the man for his insensitivity. The woman was pale, but conscious.

"Go and get her some water," Rachel ordered the man, who looked suitably chastised. She supported the woman and moved her away from the crowd while the other woman who had been a part of the conversation pulled up a chair for her.

"Are you alright, Glenis?"

"I will be in a moment, thanks to this young lady."

The other woman turned to Rachel. She looked to be in her late seventies, had a blue-rinse perm, wore silver-rimmed spectacles, and was elegantly dressed in spite of the t-shirt beneath the smart tailored trouser suit.

"Thank you."

"That's alright. It looks like you've all had a shock."

The man returned with a glass of water and a tray of tea, which he placed on a nearby table. "I'm sorry, Mrs Blunt – Glenis – I can be a bit blunt at times." His attempt at humour brought a smile to Glenis's face. "It's my military background, you know? I forget sometimes how to treat the fairer sex." He looked apologetically at Rachel.

"Army?" she asked.

"Forty years. Served all over the world, saw some things…"

"Ah hmm." Rachel nodded towards the recovering lady before he decided to elaborate.

"Well, yes. Anyway, let me pour some tea. Would you like to join us?"

"Thank you, I will." They moved over to the table where the tray had been placed.

"Who do I thank for saving me?" The woman called Glenis enquired.

"My name's Rachel, Rachel Prince, and I hardly saved you. The floors are hard, though, if you fall on them." Rachel flinched as she remembered one of her own previous experiences.

"Pleased to meet you, Rachel. This is Prudence Crowther and I'm Glenis Blunt."

"And I'm Charles Crane, at your service, Miss."

"Are you on a tour?" Rachel asked, despite knowing they were.

"Yes, we're on an international bucket list tour organised by the travel agency owned by the poor dead woman. All the people wearing these t-shirts are. Most of us met in Adelaide yesterday, stayed overnight in an overpriced hotel, and now we're on this cruise for two weeks. A few of the group only arrived today and I haven't met everyone myself yet. I do hope we don't have to return to port."

"They can't do that, Prudence, we've paid good money to be here," snorted Charles.

"But a woman has died." Glenis paled again.

"Yes, well she probably won't be the last either, considering our average age is eighty plus."

"I think it's more likely that the unfortunate lady will be repatriated to port from the ship because the cruise line won't want to wait until we reach Melbourne, the next big city. I don't believe Kangaroo Island would be a suitable place, and we've not long set sail anyway so

Adelaide is nearer." Rachel surmised this was what would be likely to happen rather than knowing.

"Was it an accident?" Prudence asked. "Or a heart attack?"

Charles coughed as if not wanting to answer. He lowered his voice. "From what I hear, it was murder."

Rachel grimaced at the word and immediately had flashbacks to her previous cruises. *Why does this always happen to me?*

The others continued speaking in whispered tones while Rachel sipped her tea thoughtfully.

"Probably the son."

Charles's voice brought Rachel back to the present and she tuned into the conversation again.

"What makes you say that?" she asked.

"Rumour has it that Mrs F still owned the business and was in charge of the purse strings. That new wife of his is costing him a fortune, but Mrs F liked to be in control."

"How do you know all this?" asked Prudence.

"I was sitting in the hotel bar late last night. Flanders was drunk and complaining to a couple of guys who had dropped by from the travel agency with some last minute instructions. I heard them talking – he said that he wished she was dead and feared she was going to live forever. He'd tried to keep her off this tour, said he wanted some space, but his mother was having none of it. The guys were ribbing him about his young wife, and then they changed the subject. I didn't think anything of it at the time, put it down to normal family bickering, and having met the woman, couldn't blame him, but now – well, who knows? He would be my number one suspect if I were investigating."

"I'm most relieved to hear it's a family matter." Glenis, who had been making a remarkable recovery, brightened even more. "I'd hate to think we had a killer among us."

"Oh, I hadn't even thought of that," said Prudence.

"On the other hand, it could be an ageist serial killer." Thankfully Glenis and Prudence were too busy nattering to hear Charles's latest attempt at inappropriate humour.

Rachel filed the conversation away in her brain. She too would be happy for it to simply be a matter of a family feud. The crime would be quickly solved and she wouldn't have to be involved. She had observed the aggressive new chief of security enter the library and wasn't keen for their paths to cross anytime soon.

It hadn't taken long for the group she'd met, which had gradually grown to half a dozen, to move on from the demise of Mrs F to more light-hearted conversation.

"That's why it was called a bucket list cruise," a rather brash woman from South Africa quipped. "I knew someone would have to die – makes it more exciting, don't you think?" The only one who engaged with the woman was Charles, having found a likeminded passenger with the same morbid humour.

After hanging around for a while outside the library with the friendly group, Rachel felt it was time she made a move.

"It's been a pleasure meeting you all. I do hope the rest of your cruise is uneventful, in the nicest possible way."

"Oh, it will be an adventure if the first few hours are anything to go by," answered Charles. "Don't worry, I'll look after these ladies."

That's what I was concerned about, thought Rachel. "Then I'm sure they'll be in safe hands." She winced as she said it.

"Thank you again for saving me, Rachel," called Glenis as Rachel crossed over to the other side of the ship. She waved a hand in acknowledgement and continued her journey.

Rachel remained long enough to see Sarah and the medical team move out of the library with a trolley stretcher carrying a body that she presumed was Mrs F. Sarah had been too preoccupied to notice her – perhaps as well as she wouldn't like the idea of Rachel snooping. The chief of security, identified by the number of gold stripes on his epaulettes, left shortly after the medical team. Locked in conversation with Jason Goodridge, Sarah's beau, the chief looked none too pleased with proceedings. He waved his arms around, barking out instructions to security guards and any poor crew member who happened to be in the vicinity.

The bumptious man was around five foot seven, Rachel assessed, and at least three sizes too large for his stature. He was younger than Waverley, perhaps late thirties, with crew cut blond hair. Rachel wondered if he originated from Scandinavia. The uniform clung tightly to his portly belly with his belt struggling to hold the trousers up underneath the overhang. She suspected he would be wearing braces underneath the jacket. His pale face was flushed with anger or stress, Rachel wasn't sure which.

Jason was listening patiently to the barrage of instructions being fired at him, and finally, the chief bustled away. Afterwards a tall, spindly man wearing a pink turban also exited the library, looking distressed. It was this man Rachel was heading towards now.

She found him seated alone on the opposite side of the deck to the library: port side, she gathered from the direction the ship was travelling in. He was staring out to sea.

"The sea is so calm, isn't it?" Rachel commented casually.

The man looked up, his pale brown eyes dull as he replied. "It is indeed so. I wish it were as calm on board ship. I've just witnessed a terrible incident."

"Oh dear, I'm sorry to hear that. Was it the lady in the library?"

"Ah, news has already spread, I see."

"I've just been with a few of the group she was travelling with. I see you are a member too."

He looked bashfully down at his t-shirt, not at all in keeping with the rest of his smart attire. "I apologise for my tawdry look, I usually wear suit and tie." As if to prove it, he motioned to the smart white jacket hanging neatly over the back of a chair.

Rachel smiled. She liked this quiet and unassuming man with his turban, long well-groomed beard and bushy moustache. "Where are you from?" she asked.

"I'm from the Punjab, but I was educated in Oxford. You are English I take it? My name is Manandeep Janda, but my friends call me Deep."

"That explains your perfect English accent. I thought you were English for a moment," said Rachel. "I'm Rachel Prince, and yes, English. My parents live in Hertfordshire, I work in London."

"Is this your first cruise, Miss Prince?"

"Please call me Rachel. No, it's my fourth, but my first time in these parts."

"Being from a land-locked part of India, I've always wanted to do something like this," he said. "My family think I've lost my marbles, but then, many of them have never travelled at all."

"Are you taking the cruise alone, or is your wife with you?"

"Alone in some senses, but with forty odd others tagging along. I'm broadening my horizons, sharing a room with an English Buddhist convert. I'm a Sikh so it will make the tour all the more enlightening."

"I know what you mean. My father's a vicar and he shared a dorm with a follower of Hare Krishna when he was at university. In spite of many heated discussions, they remain friends to this day."

"Would your father not have studied at a Bible college?"

"He did go to theological college, but his first degree was in philosophy. He went to your opposite number, Cambridge!" She smiled apologetically.

Rachel found Deep easy to talk to and could have chatted to him for hours. He was like her father in many ways, although thirty years older. Understanding and respectful, he listened and processed information before offering an opinion.

An hour had whizzed by and she hadn't asked him a single question about the murder. It was getting late and she felt sure Deep would miss his dinner if she kept him talking for much longer.

"I'd better let you get your dinner," she said.

Deep looked at his watch. "Is that the time already? I would have liked to change for dinner, but out of respect for Florence, I'll keep the t-shirt on." His shoulders drooped.

"Was that the lady who died?"

"Yes, she was an old friend – from another life – much too long ago to go back to." He spoke whimsically with a faraway look in his eyes. Sighing deeply, he stood to shake Rachel's hand. "It's been an absolute pleasure, Rachel Prince. I do hope we'll meet again."

"I hope so too, Deep." She watched as he turned and walked away slowly. Rachel kicked herself for not asking more questions, but then reminded herself that the death was nothing to do with her; not her investigation.

As if that's going to work! her inner voice said sarcastically.

Chapter 6

"I knew things would hot up now your Rachel's on board, Sarah, but I really wasn't expecting another murder," Brigitte complained after they had transferred the body to the morgue as a temporary measure.

"It's worse than that. She was with me when I got the emergency call, now she's bound to ask what it was all about." Sarah flopped down on to a comfy chair in senior nurse Gwen Sumner's office.

Alex came into the room, followed by Bernard. Graham and Gwen were last to arrive as they had had the unenviable task of tracking down the woman's son.

"How did he take it?" asked Sarah.

"To be honest, he was rather dismissive, almost brash. All but told us these things happen at her age and he'd been surprised she'd lived as long as she had. He looked rather chipper, as a matter of fact. I nearly put my foot in it, thinking his wife was his daughter, but thankfully Gwen intervened and saved any embarrassment."

"Did he realise his mother had been stabbed?" asked Brigitte, shocked.

"To be fair, not for a while because he kept interrupting after Graham told him his mother had been found dead in the library. His wife, who is roughly the same age as his daughter, just carried on polishing her nails without a care in the world. I wouldn't have realised she was his wife either if I hadn't been carrying printouts of the family's files. You should have seen what she was wearing."

"Quite," interrupted Graham, keen to get back on track. "And murder wasn't the first thing I thought of mentioning, but after a few of his rants, I had to cut in and tell him that his mother had not died of natural causes and that someone, in all likelihood, had murdered her."

"Strange thing, the odd man then suggested it must have been suicide! Before Graham got to say anything else, the new CSO, Brian Heel, walked in and all but told us to get out."

"I'll be having words with him later about his attitude," said Graham. "We can't be having him speaking to people like that, not to mention the fact he doesn't outrank me, except in matters of security, of course. He will be getting a piece of my mind."

Graham Bentley was a placid man generally, but very protective of the medical team and a stickler for etiquette. Sarah almost felt sorry for the new security chief, but then felt he had it coming to him. He'd been hostile in the library and unnecessarily brusque with passengers as well as barking at Jason, so he wasn't going to get too much support from her.

"Anyway, there's something else I need to mention," added Graham. "Let's have a drink first."

Raggie, the medical team steward, had left pots of tea and coffee along with pastries for them when he heard they had been called to an emergency. Once they were all settled, Graham sipped his coffee.

"There's an odd mark on the woman's ankle. If I didn't know better, I'd say it was a snakebite."

The gasps in the room were loud.

"I know it sounds strange, and I need to take a closer look at the body, but I came across a lot of snakebites when I worked in the Bush in Australia as a young doctor, and one doesn't forget these things. What do you think, Gwen?"

"I haven't seen the mark but I'm native to these parts and not unfamiliar with snakebites, so I'll gladly take a look. Personally, though, you could well be right. I certainly don't think she died of a stab wound."

"But the blood?" said Sarah.

"I agree with Gwen. I know it looked like a lot of blood, but it wasn't enough to have caused her death. Also the knife wound was small, neither deep enough nor in the right place to cause the woman's death. There were no defensive wounds either; you don't just let someone stab you in the chest without putting up a fight." Graham took a slurp of coffee after his explanation.

"I did wonder about that myself," added Bernard. "I worked in casualty in Manila and we saw hundreds of stab wounds – there is a lot of violence in my country. I was surprised about this one too. I was going to ask you about it."

"Good man – see, team, we have the best medics on the high seas," Graham announced proudly, to which Bernard responded with a cheeky grin.

"Before we continue with this back-slapping commentary, I think you're missing something." Gwen walked towards the phone.

"What's that?" asked Graham.

"If you are right, there's a venomous snake on board the *Coral Queen*."

"Goodness me, Gwen! You're right. We'd better inform the captain. I'll let him tell the obnoxious Brian Heel." Graham left the room and Gwen called through to Guest Services to have staff be on the lookout for a potentially missing reptile.

"Come on, Sarah, you're with me," Gwen instructed as she collected a glass container. The box was carried onboard as a precaution, to house severed limbs should the worst occur to one of the staff or crew who worked with large machinery and potentially dangerous implements. Thankfully, Sarah had never seen it used for its true purpose, and as the container still had a manufacturer's label attached, she was reassured that it had not been required to date.

The library was still sealed off and Graham arrived ahead of them.

"There are so many places the blighters can hide in a room like this. It could be under one of the bookcases or in any one of a hundred hidden corners," Gwen informed them.

"Are you sure we should be doing this?" asked Sarah, who was suddenly developing a fear of snakes that hadn't been present before this moment.

"We'll just hang around," suggested Graham. "I've requested a vet join the lifeboat coming to collect the body. Hopefully, our serpent will stay put until he or she arrives, but we can't let a snake get loose among passengers."

"Let's hope it isn't already," said Sarah, looking cautiously around her, understanding their duty of care, but remaining ill at ease. The majority of passengers would be at first sitting for dinner or attending the first theatre show, and those that did stray near were being diverted to the opposite side of the deck by a security guard.

Loud footsteps and an even louder voice could be heard approaching.

"Heel," groaned Graham.

"What do you mean by commandeering my officers who should be investigating a murder?" The small obese man spat the words out at Graham, who was momentarily taken aback.

"Control yourself, man, you're creating a scene." Graham spoke quietly, but the assertive tone, developed over many years' experience of working under extreme stress, was unmistakeable.

Heel came to heel immediately.

Typical playground bully, thought Sarah as Graham sat the officer down, and explained his findings and his suspicions.

"Right," the bumptious man said at last. "I'll, erm, leave you to deal with the reptile then. I have things to attend to, passengers to interview. Let me know when it's found. At least that rules out murder." On seeing Sarah, he stopped in his tracks and paused. He glared harshly as if about to say something, but Graham intervened.

"You'd better be on with it, then. Snakes can appear very suddenly from nowhere, you know."

"Right, oh, yes. You're right, I should get on." Heel almost ran down the corridor.

"Coward," sneered Gwen.

"Indeed. What was that all about, Sarah? Do you know him?" Graham's brow furrowed.

"No, the first I saw of him was earlier when I was comforting the passenger who had tried to resuscitate the unfortunate victim. I think I'd remember him if I had met him in the past, not someone I'd be likely to forget. You know what it's like in our profession, though. I could have come across him if he was ever a patient or a relative of a patient." She thought for a moment. "No, I don't think so. Unless he knows I'm dating one of his security team, I have no idea what his problem is."

"If looks could kill, though – what's more, why would he presume it's no longer murder?" asked Gwen.

"Quite. Of course it's still a suspicious death, she hardly stabbed herself. Very strange man; if I didn't know better—"

Graham didn't get to finish his sentence as Sarah hastily stood and stared at a three-foot long bluish-black snake with white stripes slithering towards them.

Gwen was the first to react as Sarah stood open mouthed, stifling a scream. The experienced senior nurse took the lid off the container they had brought and laid it down on the floor, then grasped the reptile's head with a small pair of baby delivery forceps, forcing the rest of its body into the box before finally squashing the creature's head in and releasing the forceps at the last minute. Sarah had the foresight to slam the lid down immediately Gwen let go.

A security officer, who had joined them, replaced the taser on to his belt.

"Well done, Gwen," said Graham, looking slightly ashen. "That's our killer right there. I wonder how it got on board."

Gwen sat down for a moment, breathless and trembling slightly from the adrenaline release. "That's no Australian snake. I've never seen anything like that."

"It looks quite pretty in the box. I can't understand why, if the snake is the killer, Mrs F was also stabbed?" announced Sarah, realising her hands were also trembling.

"Yes, that bit doesn't make any sense at all. Anyway, let's get this creature out of here before any of the passengers get wind of it." Gwen covered the case with her uniform jacket, dispensing with ship's uniform rules. "I think I'll be forgiven this once," she said, smiling.

Chapter 7

Rachel followed the waiter into the Coral Restaurant as he led her towards a table set for one.

"Rachel!"

She froze with dread in recognition of the voice calling out to her from a table nearby. Spinning around, she looked into the face of her ex-fiancé. Here stood the man who had caused her so much pain a couple of years ago.

"Robert." Her voice faltered, all the raw emotions she had felt before resurfacing.

Seemingly oblivious to her discomfort, or more likely not caring, he continued, "How good to see you again. You look beautiful." He leaned forward and kissed her on the cheek before she gathered herself enough to move away.

"What are you doing here?" She inwardly kicked herself for sounding so feeble, feeling even more foolish that her hands were trembling at the sight of him. Without waiting for an answer, she turned away from him and back to the waiter. "I'm sorry, I need to go. I'm keeping this man waiting." Robert's eyes followed her gaze towards the waiter, and worse still, the table for one he was leading her to. The conceited smirk betrayed how pleased he was that she seemed to be alone.

"Rachel, there you are! Please join us at our table. We've been waiting for you." Deep winked at the waiter. "I think there's been some mistake. Miss Prince is joining us for dinner." Before she knew what was happening, her new saviour took hold of her elbow and escorted her to a round table for eight people a little way away from where Robert was sitting.

"Thank you." Her voice was still trembling.

"It's nothing. I hope you don't mind my interfering, but you seemed uncomfortable. Was that man bothering you? You look unwell. Can I pour you a drink?"

Rachel saw the bottles of wine on the table.

"Red wine, please." She worked hard to compose herself while Deep poured the wine, and she was pleased when a large lady to his left engaged him in conversation. Her heart was still pounding and she felt dizzy.

Deep soon turned his attention back towards her. "Who is he?"

"Someone I used to know." Fighting back the tears stinging her eyes, she took a large sip of wine.

"Forgive me. I don't mean to pry, but I would say that's someone you used to love."

"Yes, he is. Like you and Mrs F, I suspect?" The faraway look in his eyes told Rachel she was right and it helped bring her back to her senses.

"That was a long time ago."

"I suspect you still loved her, though."

"Sometimes we love the memories that we create in our heads rather than those that are a true reflection, I think."

"That's deep, Deep. You know, I think you're right. Thank you for that pearl of wisdom. Are you sure you don't mind me joining you for dinner?"

"On the contrary, you're easy to talk to and perhaps it will help me forget the awful events of earlier."

Rachel had almost forgotten about the body in the library. She shook her head briskly to dismiss the shock of running into her ex here of all places. All through dinner, she surreptitiously glanced over to where Robert sat with his back to her. She recognised one of the men with him from the police force where he worked in Manchester. He was sitting at a table for six, and judging by the way they were engaging in animated conversation, they all knew each other. There was an older woman in her early forties, a young woman, mid-twenties, and a beautiful woman a few years older than Rachel. Wearing a blue sari, she sat immediately next to Robert with another man on her right.

"Are you going to tell me who he is?" asked Deep gently.

"My ex-fiancé. I haven't seen him since he broke off the engagement two years ago."

"The man's a fool," said Deep.

"I'll drink to that." Rachel picked up her wine glass and clinked glasses with her new friend.

"I suspect you are still a little in love with him, perhaps."

"No, I'm in love with the man waiting for me in London. His name is Carlos." She wondered why she sounded so defensive and why her heart was still pounding at the sight of Robert being so close. "As you suggested, perhaps I'm in love with the good memories. It's just a shock seeing him, that's all. He works, or did work, in Manchester when we were engaged."

"Why did he break off the engagement, if you don't mind telling an old man?"

Rachel found herself telling Deep how they had met when she was a police probationer working in Leeds and how Robert had swept her off her feet, asked her to marry him, and then, out of the blue, taken her out to lunch to break off the engagement.

"He found someone else, told me he was in love and was going to marry her. That's the last I heard. I didn't take it very well, walked away and refused all contact with him afterwards. He kept trying to phone me for months, but I blocked him from calling my mobile or texting, and then he wrote a letter."

"What did the letter say?"

"I don't know, I never read it. I met Carlos a few months later and we've been together ever since." The thought of Carlos made her feel warm and safe again, but she couldn't push away the effect that bumping into Robert had had on her.

"I didn't see a wedding ring on his finger. I think you had better be careful, Rachel. From the way he looked at you, I would say he might be going to try to get you back. Let me tell you one thing about men like him. It's all about the chase."

Rachel gulped, wishing she was anywhere but on this cruise. *How dare he come aboard the precious ship she loved so much and disrupt her life like this.* She picked at her food throughout dinner, politely listening but not hearing the conversations around her.

It wasn't until halfway through the meal that she realised Prudence was sitting opposite her, next to Glenis Blunt and the insensitive Charles, all of whom she'd met earlier. On hearing Charles's voice, she realised she had been staring down at her food for at least forty minutes.

"I still think the son did it." Charles's words dragged Rachel from her pity party, and she looked up and noticed the other people around the table. A polite, demure man sat to Rachel's right, next to Charles who he had mainly spoken with throughout dinner. To Deep's left was a large woman who looked around eighty years old, and she was next to a woman resembling a stick insect who remained upright and spoke mainly to Glenis on her left.

"I don't really want to talk about it," said Deep abruptly. "If you'll excuse me." He stood up, nodding courteously towards Rachel and the woman on his left before leaving the restaurant.

"Now look what you've done," scolded Prudence.

"Sorry, I'll make it up to him later. We're meeting for a game of Blackjack in the casino. He told me he plays and I thought it might cheer him up – he had quite a shock." Charles obviously meant no harm, but didn't know when to stop.

"It's lovely to see you again, Rachel. Will you join us for dinner every evening?" Glenis looked pleadingly at Rachel, who supposed the poor woman might need sheltering from the force that was Charles, and she herself might need sheltering from the other force that was Robert.

"I'm not sure about every night, but if I can, I will."

"Come along, ladies, it's time for the show." The man who had been sitting next to Rachel spoke up.

"Will you come too, Rachel?" asked Prudence

"Thank you, but I'm meeting a friend shortly. Perhaps another time."

Rachel noticed out of the corner of her eye Robert leaving with the attractive Asian woman whispering in his ear. The woman glared at Rachel as they passed by. Robert was distracted by the man Rachel had recognised, who nodded to her.

"You're welcome to him," Rachel muttered after the Asian woman. On allowing a few minutes to pass, she herself left the restaurant feeling totally drained.

As soon as she entered the Jazz Bar, the relaxed atmosphere calmed her nerves. The familiar feel of the room and the rhythmic music relieved the tension and helped her control the tumultuous thoughts racing around in her head.

She felt a tap on her shoulder and jumped, fists clenched.

"Rachel, it's me. Sorry, did I startle you?" Sarah hugged her.

"No, sorry, I'm a bit jumpy."

Sarah stared at the clenched fists but said nothing. They found a quiet booth away from the crowds.

"What will you have?" asked Sarah.

"Martini and lemonade, please. I'm sorry about before – I'm not feeling right."

"What's the matter, Rachel? You look like you've seen a ghost."

"I might as well have. Guess who I ran into in the dining room tonight?"

"Not another ex-criminal vowing vengeance, please?"

"No, worse, it was Robert."

"Robert as in ex-fiancé scumbag, Robert?"

Rachel laughed. "That's the one."

Sarah frowned, concerned. "Was his wife with him?"

"That's the thing, he wasn't even wearing a ring, and he had an Asian woman hanging on his every word. I'm sure the woman he left me for was called Jessica, hardly an Asian name."

"Mm, well if that's the case, you had a lucky escape – he's clearly not to be trusted. Rachel, please tell me you're not still in love with him? What about Carlos?"

"I'm not – at least I don't think I am, but I do admit to feeling confused. My heart's only just stopped pounding after seeing him again. Perhaps it's the shock. I do love Carlos. You can't be in love with two people, can you?"

"No, Rachel. Some people might be able to be, but not you. You're a one-man woman, and trust me, Carlos is that man."

"I'm sure you're right." The drinks arrived and Rachel picked up her Martini, looking at the worried scowl on her best friend's face. Although Sarah had never said anything, Rachel suspected that Robert had tried to drive a wedge between them. In fact, he'd driven a wedge between her and everyone else she knew. It was time to talk about something else.

"I heard about the murder."

"I don't know how you do it, Rachel Prince. No sooner are you on board this ship than there's a murder!"

"Well, I know who I'd like to murder right now." Rachel took another sip of her drink.

"Don't let him get to you, he doesn't deserve you – never did. Moving on from the subject of scumbag, how did you hear about the murder, and do you know who it was?"

"No, I haven't had time to track the killer down yet."

Both women giggled. "You know that's not what I meant." Sarah looked around to check no-one was listening in. "It was our Mrs F."

"I did know. After you left, I couldn't resist coming down to the library and hanging around outside. I got talking to a few people from the bucket list tour, and before you know it, I was told the full story. Then I managed to speak with the man who found her, Deep Janda. He's a lovely man, makes me think of the grandfather I never knew. He also rescued me in the dining room after Robert accosted me."

"Wow! All in the space of a few hours, that has to be a record. I just can't leave you alone, can I? I bet you don't know how she died, though." Sarah lowered her voice again and took a drink of Chardonnay.

"Yes, I do, a man called Charles told us she was stabbed."

"Ah-hah, for once, PC Prince, you're wrong. The stab wound was too superficial, according to Graham who also noticed marks on her ankle."

"What sort of marks?"

"A bite – your turn to guess."

"Well it can't have been a vampire if it was her ankle, so it must have been a spider or a snake. My money's on a snake?"

Sarah let out a deep sigh. "Right as usual, Miss Clever Clogs. No-one likes a smart alec, you know. It was a venomous snake. Gwen caught it – you should have seen her, Rachel, she was amazing. It's been collected by a vet and taken back to Adelaide, along with the body of the late Mrs F who will have a post mortem tomorrow morning. The vet has identified the snake as an Indian krait, highly toxic, gives off a powerful neurotoxin causing muscle paralysis she says. The vet will test the snake to see if it is still venomous, so all we need to find out now is how it got on board, and who stabbed poor Mrs F after she was bitten."

"We? I thought you didn't like me getting involved?"

"I don't, but I don't trust the new security chief, Brian Heel. What's more, he was horrible to Jason and glared at me like I was his sworn enemy. Graham thinks I've met him before, Gwen says I need to be careful, but I don't know who he is other than our interim security chief. I've never seen him before, but he seems to know me."

"That's disturbing, I hope you're not in danger." Rachel couldn't bear the thought of having to worry about Sarah as well as avoiding her ex.

"He probably doesn't know me from Adam. I bet he's got wind of the fact that I'm dating a member of the security team and for some reason – most likely because he's a killjoy – he doesn't like it."

"That makes more sense. He certainly looked to me like he wouldn't want anyone to be happy."

After an hour, Rachel felt much more like her old self, and after saying goodnight to Sarah, she made her way back to her room with a plan in mind. Investigating and solving the murder would be the best thing to keep her occupied. It would help her stay out of trouble.

Chapter 8

After a restless night's sleep, Rachel pulled on her gym trousers, sweatshirt and trainers, deciding to take a run around the track on deck sixteen. The early morning sunshine was burning its way through light peppery clouds – a spring day off the south-west Australia coast was like a summer's day in England, but it seemed odd experiencing spring in October.

The morning temperature would be comfortable for her run and switching to music on her iPhone while putting her earpieces in place heralded the start of her morning routine, beginning with stretches. The only time the routine changed was when she pulled in night shifts, and then things switched around to accommodate sleeping during the day.

Her thoughts during the night had been dominated by the shock meeting with Robert. *Why hadn't he looked surprised?*

The battle within her had raged through the night. On the one side was her love for Carlos, and on the other, renegade memories daring to surface of the happy times she remembered with Robert.

Yes, the Robert who dumped you.

Finally sense had prevailed and the emotions were brought under control. A couple of years had passed since she had last seen her ex, with their final conversation resulting in her storming out of a café after he'd told her about his new relationship. Since then, she had completely blocked him and any contact with him from her life. It had helped her survive the darkest days of her young life, and during the night, she realised with considerable relief that after the initial shock of seeing him again, she had no feelings for him.

Turning up the volume of *Hello* by Adele, she began her run.

An hour later, Rachel had showered, visited the buffet for breakfast, and was now waiting in the main atrium for Sarah who had the day off. They planned to visit the town of Penneshaw on Kangaroo Island as this was closest to where the ship had anchored. While she waited, her thoughts mulled over the murder of the unfortunate Mrs F the previous day.

"Good morning, you're looking better." Sarah pulled her into a hug and beamed.

"I feel better, thanks. Cleared my head with a morning run and got things back in perspective."

"Sure?"

"Yep, positive. It was just the shock of seeing scumbag, as you call him."

The young women laughed as they made their way to queue for a tender in order to leave the ship. The waters were too shallow to dock and the ship had dropped anchor early this morning. As they stood arm in arm, Rachel watched, fascinated, as the small tenders were released from the ship and saw them docking alongside a lengthy pier-like structure a mile or so away.

Sarah was wearing mufti as she was off duty and looked radiant. Jason had brought the light back into her friend's life and Rachel couldn't be more pleased for her. Friends since childhood, they had been through good and bad times at school, followed by university where they'd shared halls and then a flat, and through it all they had remained best friends forever. Rachel missed Sarah when she started working for the cruise line, leaving their flat in Leeds. But, she realised now, Robert had worked hard at separating them, something Rachel hadn't recognised while under the dazzling influence of the man who at the time was the love of her life. The man she had planned to spend the rest of her life with.

"Come on, Rachel, snap out of it or you'll miss your footing."

Her friend was right, but thankfully two members of crew stood either side to assist passengers and off-duty crew into the tender boats that were packed solid with excited people.

"Sorry, I was just appreciating our long and trusty friendship. I really like Jason, Sarah. Is it serious?"

"We're taking it slowly, but I think it is, yes." The light in her eyes said it all. "What about you and Carlos? I bet Marjorie's growing impatient you're not engaged yet."

Marjorie was the elderly woman who had become closer than a grandmother to Rachel. Rachel had met Marjorie on her first cruise and she was as good a friend as anyone could wish for, in spite of the age difference.

"Ah, I've been meaning to talk to you about that!" Rachel held out her left hand to show the single diamond-studded gold ring. Sarah leapt for joy, causing a few tut-tuts from some passengers and smiles from others, and hugged her friend tight, letting out loud whoops.

"When? How? Wow, Rachel, I'm so pleased!"

They sat down again on one of the benches. Rachel had wanted to tell her friend the day before, but Sarah had been called away to the emergency, and last night would have been tainted by her encounter with Robert.

"He took me out to dinner at the top of the Shard before I left London, then in-between courses he got down on one knee. Sarah, it was magical. My heart was bursting. I had begun to think he would never ask, while at the same time being frightened he might. To be honest, it was the perfect time to do so because only that week I had decided that if he did ask, I would say yes. Divine intervention, methinks."

Rachel grinned from ear to ear. "I didn't wear the ring yesterday because I wanted to tell you privately. Of course, I did tell Marjorie before I left, and my parents already knew because, unbeknown to me, Carlos had driven up to Hertfordshire the weekend before to ask their permission. Dad is really fond of him now – you know he had doubts for a while because of how much Robert hurt me, but they have become good friends over recent months after Dad hired Carlos to investigate some lead thefts from the church roof as the police hadn't been able to find the culprits." Carlos worked as a private investigator, running his own business in London. "As you know, Carlos caught them within a fortnight, and he and Dad have been best buddies ever since. Carlos even comes to church with me when we visit my parents; he has great respect for my dad."

"What about your mum?"

"She's been a Carlos fan ever since she met him. You know how charming he can be. I'm amazed she managed to keep it secret that he was going to propose."

"Oh Rachel, I'm so happy for you, I could burst. Drinks are on me tonight."

Rachel breathed a huge sigh of relief at having told Sarah, now feeling that all was well in her world again after the turmoil of the previous night. "You know, I realised what upset me so much seeing Robert last night. It was the memory of the pain he caused, and then the fear that it could happen again. Sometimes I get this weird feeling that I'm not meant to be happy and fear

Carlos doing the same thing, especially since we got engaged."

"Well you know the answer to that on both counts. Yes, you are meant to be happy, and definitely no. Carlos. Would. Never. Do. That. To. You. He loves you, Rachel. Robert just wanted to own you; Carlos has never been like that."

"You're absolutely right, and I came to the same conclusion last night and this morning, so let's forget about scumbag, shall we?"

"You won't get any argument from me on that front!"

The next few hours were taken up with walking around Penneshaw and the surrounding area. They saw kangaroos in the wild, sea lions offshore and penguins roaming freely. Rachel found it all magical and Sarah was entranced despite having toured the island extensively on previous visits – she loved nature. The bouncy, unadulterated joy shone through her wide eyes and the pleasure she took in showing Rachel around made both of them happy.

"Do you fancy a coffee?" Rachel pointed to an outdoor beach café she liked the look of where a live band was playing. The trio was dressed in beach shorts and t-shirts, singing popular melodies from the 1950s. She realised their reason for the choice of repertoire when she saw that the café was packed with bucket list passengers. Glenis and five of her friends, minus Deep, sat at a table to the far side of the bar.

"Okay, you get drinks and I'll go and grab that table underneath the palm tree over there."

Rachel nodded and managed to fight her way to the bar, only to be told it was waiter service and to take a seat. The blond male proprietor gave her an appreciative glance before being nudged by one of the waiters.

"Keep your eyes on the job, mate."

Rachel took a menu from the bar and made her way to where Sarah was seated.

"Waiter service," she explained.

No sooner had she sat down than the blond proprietor appeared. "What can I get you beautiful girls?" he asked.

Rachel rolled her eyes and ignored his flirting. "Coffee, white, no sugar," she answered crisply.

"I'll have a cola," said Sarah.

"Coming right up." He smiled at them both, showing perfect white teeth beneath the tanned skin, and even Rachel had to laugh at how obvious he was.

"Ignore him, Rachel, he's just being friendly. Aussies are generally friendly and the men can't help themselves. Besides, he is rather attractive."

"Sarah Bradshaw, I'm surprised at you!" Rachel giggled.

Their laughter was short-lived as the figure of Robert appeared and pulled up a seat.

"That seat's taken," said Sarah, glowering at him.

"It is now," he answered, snubbing her completely and turning his chair towards Rachel. "We didn't finish our conversation last night."

"There was no conversation last night. What do you want, Robert?"

He smiled the flirtatious smile that would have once produced butterflies in her stomach. "I thought we could catch up on old times. I'm sure your friend wouldn't mind leaving us for a while."

"Right, that's it." Sarah called the good-looking proprietor over. "Would you ask this person to leave, please? He's unwelcome here."

"Right you are. Come on, mate, you heard the lady, you need to move on." He put a heavy hand on Robert's shoulder.

Robert glared at Sarah, then at the proprietor, but thankfully decided not to create a scene. He pulled on his false smile and leaned in towards Rachel, whispering, "This conversation isn't over. You know you still want me, it's written all over your face." At that moment he caught sight of the engagement ring and was momentarily caught off guard. "Catch you later."

He smirked before walking towards his group who were sitting outside a bar nearby.

"Are you okay, ladies?" The proprietor seemed genuinely concerned.

"We're fine, thank you." Sarah smiled at him sweetly. He returned to the café bar while Sarah looked at Rachel, eyes filled with worry. "Rachel, he's trouble."

Rachel was shaken to the core. "I don't ever remember him being threatening like that. A few of his friends told me he could fly off the handle with his subordinates, but I never witnessed anything like his behaviour just now. Maybe he's been drinking."

Sarah looked thoughtful. "Perhaps he was showing off to those Neanderthals." She pointed towards the two men now playing football on the beach with Rachel's ex.

The drinks arrived and Rachel was pleased to notice out of the corner of her eye Robert and his entourage moving on further along the beach. They were talking loudly, almost as if wanting to draw attention to themselves. Drinking hadn't been an issue when she'd known Robert, he'd only ever stuck to a couple of beers, but, she reasoned, perhaps she hadn't known him very well at all, seeing only what she wanted to see at the time.

"I must have been blind."

"Don't be too hard on yourself, you were in love and he swept you off your feet. You had a lucky escape there, I dread to think what he would have been like had you married him. I'm going to take a look at his records when I get back on board and find out where he's staying so you can avoid him. I'll also ask Jason to check what trips, if any, he and his friends are booked on to. If they mirror ours, we'll change them."

"Thanks, Sarah. I think that's a good idea." A feeling of dread filled Rachel's stomach as she recalled Robert's menacing tone. It sent shivers down her spine. "That's not the man I knew. It can't be – I would never have fallen for him."

Sarah took her hand reassuringly. Her look said it all, but she added, "Come on, let's forget about him."

Rachel nodded. "You're right. Let's talk about murder instead."

Chapter 9

Rachel remained thoughtful as she made her way towards the buffet for an evening meal. Sarah was working a surgery and she didn't want to have another run in with Robert in the Coral Restaurant. She was swithering between her compassionate side wanting to help her ex if he was struggling with some inner demons, and common sense telling her to stay well away. On their way back to the ship, Rachel had tried to explain this to Sarah, but her friend was unmoved, having transferred into ultra-protective mode. This was a trait that Rachel loved about her friend, but she could find it equally irritating when it concerned her.

On entering the main buffet, she accepted for the moment that Sarah was right in this instance and it would be better to avoid Robert where possible.

Rachel liked the buffet, an area that served international cuisine both day and night, with themed nights taking pre-eminence while it continued catering for every taste. There was something for everyone. Tonight appeared to be Aborigine night with waiters dressed in traditional costumes and faces sporting varieties of face painting.

After making her way over to the main Aborigine food station, she was delighted kangaroo wasn't on the menu and chose a sweet chilli crab dish along with pineapple juice before looking around for somewhere to sit. She spotted Deep sitting alone at a table, staring out at the rapidly descending evening sun sparkling over the deep blue sea.

"Do you mind if I join you?"

Deep looked up, his wistful brown eyes returning to the present.

"Rachel! How nice to see you – yes, please do. I was feeling maudlin so it would be nice to have the distraction of a beautiful young lady."

Rachel placed her food on the table, pushing her tray to the edge, and looked sympathetically at him, thinking how much frailer he looked even since yesterday.

"I'm sorry. Is the death of your friend on your mind?"

"That, and other matters, yes."

Realising he wasn't about to continue, Rachel asked, "Did you leave the ship today?"

"Yes, I toured the island on a coach with my Buddhist roommate and his friends. Joe Flanders was the guide. It really was a lovely day and the wildlife was exquisite; it's just, I couldn't get the events of yesterday out of my head. I'm thinking of ending my tour at the next stop and returning home to India. Truth be told, I should never have come in the first place. It wasn't really to see the world, I was chasing after a dream from my youth. I'm just a foolish old man, Rachel." He looked out towards the sea again and Rachel waited, recognising his need to bring his emotions back under control.

After eating a few mouthfuls of food, she proceeded gently, "I don't believe you're foolish for one minute, Deep. There's no shame in catching up with an old friend."

"Or lover?" he asked quietly.

"Or lover. I'm sure you had no intention of being unfaithful to your wife. I've only known you briefly, but you remind me of my father, and I believe when push came to shove, you would not have done anything you would be ashamed of."

"Probably not, but I am ashamed. I told my wife a cruise of Australia and New Zealand was something I'd always wanted to do, but I didn't mention Florence would be on the cruise, although I think she may have suspected something was amiss from the way she looked at me when I left."

"She knew about your past then?"

"Yes, I told her. I met Florence at university and we fell in love. I wanted to marry her, and plucked up the courage to tell my family during my final year. My father strictly forbade it. It was 1958 and things were very different back then, but even now a Sikh does not often go against his family.

"I tried to explain to Florence and we argued. She was a strong woman even back then and wouldn't let go easily. She told me I was a weak man and that I should tell my family to – well, I won't tell you what she told me to say to them. With a broken heart, I ended the relationship. In order to stop her railing against my family any further, I told her I didn't love her anymore. She never spoke to me again, until recently.

"Within a year, my father had organised an arranged marriage for me, and deeply miserable, I married my wife."

"That must have been difficult." *Nigh on impossible*, Rachel thought, unable to formulate words or imagine how painful it would have been for a young couple deeply in love to be separated so cruelly. Deep had then been forced to marry a woman he didn't love.

Deep continued his story. "It was just as difficult for my new bride. I took my anger out on her – I was a thoughtless, inattentive husband, but she was committed to me. Patiently she bore my irritation and criticism until I began to see what a cruel man I was turning out to be. I attended gurdwara – that's where we Sikhs go to worship – and studied the Guru Granth Sahib, our holy scripture. I confessed to being in love with an Englishwoman, acknowledged and accepted responsibility for cruelty to my wife – because cruelty it was. Although I would never have hurt her physically, I was draining her with my critical tongue lashings."

"What happened?"

"I realised I should look forwards and not backwards to gain good karma, and that God had given me a faithful and beautiful wife and it was time to behave like a man of privilege. I also recognised that bitterness would not only harm my family, but in the end it would lead to my own downfall, damaging myself in this life and the next more than those I was trying to get back at – most of all, my father."

"It looks like you took your inspired advice from what I see in front of me." Rachel held Deep's sorrowful gaze. "You are a good man, Deep."

"I did take this advice, reluctantly at first, but Gurpreet won me over with her love. It took time, but I fell in love with my wife. Shortly after that God rewarded us with our first son, followed by three daughters and then another son. I love my children more than words can say; only when I became a father did I understand why my father did what he did. He thought he was doing the right thing because he loved me and I would one day be the head of the family, being the oldest son. I forgave him, but I would never have done the same thing to any of my children. I allowed them to choose for themselves and we remain close. I have ten grandchildren." His eyes lit up as he concluded his story.

"So how did you get in touch with Florence again and why?"

"Last autumn, I received a Facebook friend request out of the blue from Florence Cooper – she'd used her maiden name to set up an account. I was shocked and initially ignored it, but didn't delete it. After a couple of weeks I couldn't resist the temptation, wanting to know what had happened to her over the years. I had looked briefly at her profile and seen she was living in Australia, so I thought it could do no harm."

"You accepted and became friends again?"

"Yes, she told me she was widowed and that she had a son and granddaughter. I told her about my family and we talked via private message, eventually moving over to email. My wife has never had any interest in technology so it felt like I was doing no harm."

"So when did she ask you to meet up with her?"

"About three months ago. She said she was worried about something and felt she was in danger. At first I laughed it off, thinking she was being manipulative like the Florence of old. Six weeks ago she said she needed to discuss something with me urgently as I was the only one she could trust. It sounded like she was being paranoid but, for old time's sake, I agreed to join her on this cruise. I knew we would be surrounded by other passengers so I wasn't too concerned about guilt, even though in my heart I had always wondered. You never forget your first love, do you?"

Rachel hesitated. "I suppose not." She looked out at the sun that was now setting on the horizon. Would she ever be free of Robert?

Pulling herself together, she asked, "Did she tell you what it was she wanted to talk to you about?"

"No, only that she felt she was in danger. I came up with the story of always wanting to cruise and visit Australasia, and told my family this trip would kill two birds with one stone. I knew my wife hated to travel so there was no danger of her wanting to come.

"I arrived in Adelaide the day before yesterday. Florence sent a message to my hotel room – I was sharing the room so we couldn't meet there. Not that I would have wanted to. She asked me to meet her in the library once the ship had set sail, away from prying ears on the pretext of choosing a book for a book club during the cruise.

"When I got there, I found her slumped in the chair, almost as if she was paralysed. She had been stabbed. I'm a retired doctor so my initial reaction was to try to save her while calling for help. I've gone over the scene a few times in my head and I think I disturbed someone. I sensed someone else was present, but all I saw was Florence, and in the commotion, I forgot all about that feeling. But I'm almost certain I saw a shadow run from the room, and there was an odd smell in the air."

"Cologne?"

"No, it was difficult to distinguish because I could still smell Florence's perfume: Estée Lauder, Youth Dew. She had worn it throughout her life, I think, unless she put it on for me." Deep's eyes welled up as Rachel took his hand again.

"Do you have any idea what she was afraid of, or who?"

"None, she wouldn't say. She used the separate Facebook profile to private message me prior to the trip, but said it wasn't safe. She stopped emailing. She wanted to call me, but I don't have a mobile phone and I was terrified my wife would answer if she called my home. In the end, I compromised and agreed to this trip, thinking it was either a ploy to meet up again or her imagination getting the better of her. The mind of an older person can become a tangle of mixed-up memories and imaginations."

Rachel was about to ask some more questions when she saw the pompous chief of security heading towards the table. "Oh no, don't tell me he's found out I'm looking into the murder."

Deep looked confused and glanced up as the chief stopped at their table. "Mr Janda, I'm going to have to ask you to come with me."

"I've answered all your questions, Chief, I really don't think there's anything else I can help you with."

"You need to come with me NOW, sir."

"Would you like me to come with you?" Rachel looked at Deep.

"And who might you be?"

Rachel didn't like the man's tone. "I'm Rachel, Rachel Prince."

The chief's face reddened and he almost snorted. "That won't be necessary, Miss Prince, I'll take it from here. Mr Janda, it will be better if we don't create a scene."

Chapter 10

Rachel was livid with the bombastic chief of security as she headed towards the Jazz Bar to meet Sarah. Deep had looked totally crestfallen and helpless as he'd been led away.

Sarah was already seated at a booth table deep inside the bar. There was more privacy there than out on the main floor, where the jazz band played live music and tables were packed with passengers enjoying the night out. Rachel flung herself down on the bench opposite, letting out a loud sigh.

"What's wrong with you? Please tell me you stayed away from Robert."

"What? No, it's nothing to do with Robert. I've just had the displeasure of meeting your irritating chief of security."

"Oh." Sarah looked sympathetic, but said no more to Rachel, instead calling a waiter over. "Martini and lemonade for my friend, please, and I'll have a tonic water."

"Yes, Nurse."

"How did he find out you were investigating?"

"He didn't. I was having an enlightening conversation with Deep Janda, the man who found Mrs F yesterday, when he rudely interrupted and insisted Deep go with him for further questioning."

"That doesn't sound good. Where's he taken him?"

"I don't know. I offered to accompany Deep, but as soon as the chief heard my name – I guess he's heard of me because he made it quite clear I was not welcome – he was downright rude, to be honest."

"I'm afraid that does sound like him. Even Jason's struggling to contain himself, and you know how loyal he is."

"What can he be up to, Sarah? I don't like this at all. He treated Deep like he was the prime suspect and marched him off. I'm surprised he didn't handcuff the poor man to let everyone know how important he was."

Rachel looked towards the large bag at the side of the table. "I take it you're on call?"

Sarah followed her gaze to the bag that had to accompany medical staff when they were on call as it contained all the emergency equipment they might need. "Yes, Gwen's got a migraine so I offered to take the shift for her. She says she'll return the favour tomorrow night. That's better for me in a way as sea days are always the busiest."

The drinks arrived and Rachel sipped her martini. "I'd really like to take a look inside Mrs F's room. Do you know which one she was staying in?"

"Yes, Rachel, but I'm not going to tell you. If Brian Heel catches you, there will be a riot. He's not as forgiving as Waverley and nowhere near as humble. I don't trust him any more than you do, but you can't risk getting on his bad side."

Rachel frowned as she recognised the determined look in Sarah's eyes and knew she wouldn't budge just yet.

"I expect you're right."

"You know I am, you've met him. Does he look like the kind of man who welcomes interference… erm, help?"

"But he's got the wrong man! Deep couldn't have done this, he was in love with the woman."

Sarah's eyes widened and her eyebrows hit the ceiling. "In love? Wow, that is a turn up. You'd better tell me more."

Rachel recounted the conversation she'd had with Deep over dinner: how he had known Mrs F at university, about his family forbidding the marriage, and then how she had contacted him six months ago out of the blue.

"The thing is, Sarah, she told him she was worried someone was trying to harm her. He put it down to an overactive imagination or even manipulation, but agreed to come on this cruise partly to allay her fears and partly out of curiosity at meeting up with his old flame."

"Old is the word – it must have been sixty years ago!"

"Sixty-one to be precise. Anyway, what's age got to do with it? He said you never forget your first love." Rachel sighed wistfully.

"I think that depends on your first love, but the memories aren't always positive, are they? Do you remember Liam? I'd like to forget him for oh so many reasons."

Rachel giggled as she remembered. Liam had been Sarah's first boyfriend. They had met at the youth club run by Rachel's father, who still worked in the same village parish where the girls had both grown up. He was a spindly boy with a bad case of acne, but after he'd asked Sarah out on numerous occasions, she finally agreed.

They dated for six months with Sarah explaining to Rachel and their other school and church friends that he was 'the one'. It came as a shock to Sarah when she had gone one day to surprise him down by the river where he liked to fish and found him in a lovers' embrace with Peter, a boy from the next village.

"Yes, I do remember him. I think you were the only one who was surprised."

"That's mean, but you're right. I have no idea how I missed that."

"You were angry for months afterwards, I've never seen you that mad."

"I think it was more about being used as his cover-up than about being in love. I'd started to feel something was missing, which it obviously was." They both laughed at the recollection. "So we don't all hanker after our first loves, Rachel, and you are not hankering after Robert, so forget it."

"Trust you to bring me back down to earth. Yes, that makes sense. I suppose Deep's case is different because of the cruel way in which they were forced to part from each other. It would leave one always wondering – what if? He says he has grown to love his wife, and by all accounts, Mrs F had been happily married – not that we know much about that."

"So who was she afraid of?"

"He doesn't know. They were meeting in the library that day so that she could tell him, although I think he was more interested in talking about old times. There's no way he would have murdered her, there's no motive. He was looking forward to getting to know her again through clandestine meetings during the cruise."

"It is confusing, I admit, but I don't think our Chief Heel – ooh, I've just realised how that sounds." A fit of giggles overcame them both before Sarah continued. "CSO Heel surely wouldn't have taken him away for no reason. Anyway, maybe he did just want to ask him some more questions."

"So why the aggressive approach, and why exclude me?"

"I think you know the answer to the latter, but as for the former, I think that's just the way he is. He almost knocked me over yesterday when he barged into the library like a bulldozer. Then there was his aggressive glare at me – that still bothers me, by the way. Jason says Heel knows nothing about us so it can't have been about that."

At that moment, Sarah's radio burst into life as she was called away to attend to a passenger. "Someone's forgotten their alendronic acid."

"What's that?"

"It's a tablet they take once a week to keep osteoporosis at bay and prevent fractures. It's one of the bucket listers."

Rachel was tempted to follow her friend to see what floor the bucket list passengers were staying on, supposing that as a block booking they would all be on the same deck, but she had a better idea. First she needed to change out of the casual clothes she'd worn to eat in the buffet and for meeting Sarah in the jazz bar.

Chapter 11

Jason Goodridge was struggling to find the patience to deal with his new boss. It was only Brian's second day in charge and he had already upset most of the security team, the medical team, and now he was having a go at housekeeping.

"I don't care how busy you are, I need you to find another mattress at once. If you think I'm spending one more night on that lumpy excuse for a bed, you're mistaken." His raised voice could be heard by anyone walking along the corridor. The poor Filipina room steward from housekeeping was welling up.

Her bottom lip trembled as she stood her ground. "I'm sorry, sir, I have to attend to guest bedrooms, I'm already late because my assistant is sick. If I leave my post, I lose my job." She was terrified of the security chief, but more so of Heinz Linz, the chief hotel manager who regularly carried out ad hoc inspections of staterooms.

"You and your silly little job are of no importance to me. I care about my sleep – DO YOU UNDERSTAND?"

"Sir, that's enough." Jason could stand it no longer. Heel looked about to rip him to shreds, but like all bullies he backed down when confronted – wisely, as Jason was taller and fitter than the obese, self-important security chief.

"Well you see to it then, Goodridge. Make sure I get a new mattress TONIGHT." Turning on his heels and storming up the corridor, most likely feeling he had saved face by passing on the problem to Jason, the chief bumped into Rachel Prince who had turned out of the lift area directly into his path.

"You again! Get out of my way," Jason heard the chief shout before he muscled past Rachel, who glowered after him in astonishment.

"Who the heck does that man think he is and why is he shouting at me?"

Jason looked apologetically at Rachel, but could have hugged her when she recognised that the housekeeping steward was also upset.

"Maria, are you okay?"

"Yes, ma'am, sorry, ma'am. I was just going to do your room."

"Don't you worry about me tonight, Maria, carry on with the other rooms. I've hardly been in all day."

The steward muttered, "Thank you, ma'am." Still looking close to tears, she let herself into the next room to compose herself.

"I'm sorry, Rachel," Jason lowered his voice. "Can I come in for a minute?"

"Yes, please do."

Jason breathed a sigh of relief and briefly explained what had just occurred in the corridor. He was loyal to a fault, but in this instance he was outraged by the CSO's behaviour, and Rachel, his girlfriend's best friend, was a good sounding board. He also knew she was discreet.

"How on earth did he manage to get to such a senior position? Queen Cruises is usually so meticulous in its recruitment, I always thought – apart from the odd serial killer, that is!"

She grinned at him. Jason got the joke about a previous employee, but this was no laughing matter. Discipline was everything on board a cruise ship, and especially so within the security team who were there to ensure that passengers were kept safe and crimes swiftly and efficiently dealt with.

"I'm not sure what to do – the behaviour I've been witnessing over the past twenty-four hours is unacceptable, bordering on offensive. I should report it, but I've never reported a senior officer before."

"Have you ever worked with one like Chief Heel before, though?" She grinned again at the name.

"I worked for some hard taskmasters in the army and they weren't always fair to new recruits, but we didn't have much contact with civilians – this is different." Jason couldn't get the image of the stateroom steward out of his mind. "Now he's gone and put Mr Janda under house arrest."

"I heard that, but I'm certain Deep Janda had nothing to do with the death of Mrs Flanders."

Jason agreed, although Rachel's reply told him what he already suspected: that she was surreptitiously investigating.

"And why do you think that?"

"He doesn't fit the profile of a cold-blooded killer and this was a premeditated murder. How did the snake get on board? And why would someone stab the woman after she was dead? It doesn't make sense."

"Well, we're not sure how the snake got on board, but the stabbing may have been to draw attention away from the snakebite if they wanted to make us think the death was caused by another means. It's a warped plan if there ever was one."

"What makes you say that?"

"Well, the Krait must have bitten the woman at least three to four hours before she died. According to the vet in Adelaide, the venom is highly toxic, but doesn't usually kill straight away. She would have suffered from some sort of stomach cramps, eventually leading to paralysis. The knife could have been used after the paralysis for one of two reasons."

"Which are?"

"The first reason would be to prevent an antivenom being given in time to save her by distracting anyone who found her away from the real cause of death. The second is much worse, I'm afraid—"

"That the killer wanted her to know who had done it, being conscious but paralysed." Rachel finished the sentence for him, looking shocked. "If that's the case the person hated her enough to take a huge risk of being caught."

"I'm leaning towards the first reason, Rachel. It certainly fooled Mr Janda and the medical team initially. It was only thanks to Dr Bentley's expertise that we noticed the snakebite at all. Heel thinks that Mr Janda deliberately drew the medical team's attention towards the knife attack, ensuring the poor woman was dead before help arrived."

"Or he could have been genuinely trying to help her. What if the killer had to improvise?"

"What do you mean?"

"You say that usually these snakebites take hours to take effect, but what if it worked quicker than that – possibly due to the age of the victim? The killer would have had to do something else quickly to draw the medical team's attention away from the snakebite then, wouldn't they?"

"You mean the killer wanted to take the snake away with them so no-one would know until it was too late what they were dealing with?"

"Yes, I think that's the sum of it."

"But the plan went wrong and they panicked so stabbed the poor woman."

"Deep said he felt there was someone in the library. I suspect that someone had been going to gather up the snake and get rid of it, but was disturbed when he came in."

Jason brushed his hand through his hair. Rachel had a point and his experience of his new boss didn't fill him with confidence. Perhaps Heel was jumping to the wrong conclusion.

What he didn't tell Rachel, because he had been strictly forbidden to tell anyone, was that a foldaway glass snake cage had been found in Manandeep Janda's room, hidden in a suitcase. Either the man was a complete fool or it was a plant. He knew which way Rachel would lean, but he was under orders and decided not to share this information, certain it would come out soon enough anyway.

"You could be right, Rachel, but if you're going to do any snooping, please don't let Heel find out. I wouldn't put it past him to put you in the brig for obstruction. Now I'd better go and find him a stupid mattress. I don't need to tell you that this conversation is strictly between you and me do I?"

"What about Sarah?"

"That goes without saying." He smiled as he thought of Sarah.

She has brought light back into my life after finding me in a dark place.

Chapter 12

After Jason left, Rachel changed into an evening dress and scoured the *Coral News*, a daily brochure outlining activities taking place aboard ship.

Blast! I forgot to ask Sarah what deck Robert's staying on.

Rachel made her way to the events most likely to be attended by the bucket list tour passengers. After discovering she was on the right track following visits to the first two venues, but not seeing Charles, Prudence or Glenis, she decided she'd give one more venue a try. If unsuccessful, she'd give up for the night.

The Stars Ballroom on deck five was host to a passenger singing competition. A man in his late sixties was performing a decent rendition of *My Way* with the sound spilling over into the corridor as Rachel was heading that way. The ballroom was packed, but she couldn't immediately see anyone she recognised. Secure in the knowledge that it wouldn't be Robert's thing, she made her way through the crowds to the bar and ordered a drink.

After loud applause for the Frank Sinatra performer, she heard the unmistakable booming voice of Charles

Crane coming from the left-hand side of the stage. Although the room was dimly lit with atmospheric lighting, she saw the party she was looking for, the only problem being that there were around fifteen of the tour group gathered together in small clusters around tables, including the man who had just performed. Deciding to be brave, she ambled over to where they were sitting, carrying her drink in the hope that they would call her.

It worked.

"Rachel!" Glenis was the first to call out, followed by waves of encouragement to join them from Prudence and Charles. Deep wasn't there because Chief Heel – she liked the name and that's how she would refer to him from now on – was probably still questioning him in-between upsetting room stewards and passengers.

"Hello," she said shyly, wondering how to proceed having made no plan but to track the bucket listers down.

"Oh Rachel, do join us. I've just been telling Victor here how you saved me from fainting yesterday." The man who had sat next to Rachel at the bucket listers' dinner table was now sitting next to Glenis. He had a reddish beard with grey roots, moustache and fascinatingly bushy eyebrows that seemed to merge into one straight line.

He smiled. "I hear you were quite the heroine."

"Hardly!" Rachel was embarrassed by the attention – this certainly wasn't part of the plan, whatever the plan might have been, but a number of the group were looking her way.

"She's rather beautiful, isn't she? If only I were thirty years younger." Loud guffaws rang out as one of the men to her right spoke to the crowd on his table while looking admiringly at Rachel.

More like sixty years younger, she thought, but smiled, grimacing at the joke.

"Ignore him, Rachel, he's a dirty old man," said Prudence, her spectacles hanging around her neck on a chain. She raised a finger of warning to the gentleman in question while fluttering her eyelashes at him at the same time.

Rather long eyelashes, too. *Either they have grown considerably since we met yesterday or they are false.*

"Come and sit with us. Squash up, Charles."

"This is my friend, Rachel Prince," declared Glenis proudly. "You watch your step, Charles."

Rachel gladly sat down and people went back to their conversations now that the novelty of her presence had worn off. Their attention was drawn to the stage as an elegant looking woman in a dazzling red dress with sequins front and back began *Hey Big Spender.* The men in the group were entranced and ogled admiringly as she performed all the Shirley Bassey moves.

"Not bad for seventy-nine, is she? This is such fun," said Prudence. "I'm going to give it a go soon. Tonight is 'open mic' and tomorrow the competition starts more seriously."

"Pru is very good, I hear," encouraged Victor.

"What do you sing?" asked Rachel.

"Opera, darling. I'm a huge fan, still perform in the local operatic society back home."

"Yes, Pru lives in Sydney, but is as British as you and me," remarked Glenis.

Charles wasn't paying any attention as he was smitten with the woman on stage.

"Is the lady who's singing part of your tour party then?"

"Yes, she is. She's sitting with that group over there, all from South Africa," answered Glenis.

Rachel saw a mixed-sex group of eight sitting together, and she let out a satisfied grin. Her father had campaigned for years against Apartheid and had been over the moon when Nelson Mandela was released from prison. He would love the integrated scene playing out here.

"Who's that man on the table next to them with the young women?" She had already guessed but wanted confirmation.

"That's Joe Flanders." Charles was back with them now that the red-dressed bombshell had returned to her seat. "He's the son of the unfortunate dead woman."

"Yes and he doesn't look very sad, does he?" said Victor, glaring over at the man who was laughing loudly while taking a gulp of whiskey.

"He's had too much of this stuff again," remarked Charles, holding up his own two-thirds full glass.

"That's the wife on his right," whispered Prudence, "and the daughter on his left."

Both women were dressed in evening cocktail dresses but there the similarity ended. The wife, a busty bleach-blonde, was laughing raucously while drinking what looked like the evening's speciality cocktail, and the daughter, a rather plain looking girl about Rachel's age, sat sullenly staring at the mobile phone in her hand, blocking out the surrounding company. Rachel thought they both looked late twenties. Joe looked to be late fifties – she thought Sarah might have told her he was fifty-seven.

"Young Georgia doesn't look happy, though. I expect she's feeling the loss of her grandmother," said Glenis.

"I doubt that," said Charles, muscling in with the brash manner he had shown yesterday. "From what I hear, they were always at loggerheads. In fact I think they all wanted rid of the old lady, and now look what's happened."

"Well I have news on that front." Another woman who'd been on the dinner table the night before joined their table, having overheard the conversation. All eyes swivelled round to take in what she had to say, but they had to wait while she found space for her rather large frame.

Once seated, she pulled and straightened the dress that was clearly too tight a fit. The men were getting a little too much view of bosom as the revealing dress and the thrusting forwards and backwards to get comfortable caused it to bounce up and down, until the offending items finally rested on a roll of belly fat. Victor had discreetly looked away, but Charles ogled, finding it all very amusing from what Rachel could detect. The process took a considerable amount of time and the silence would have been deafening if Prudence hadn't taken to the stage at that moment and belted out a female version of *Nessun Dorma*. All eyes then turned away from the woman, who huffed at being ignored while the bucket listers watched their friend perform.

"Tell us in a minute, Patty," said Glenis, patting the angry looking woman's hand.

Patty sniffed and ordered a drink while looking disinterestedly towards the stage, clearly not happy at having her thunder stolen by the unassuming Prudence Crowther. Rachel listened to the song while glancing around at people on the other tables, where more and more of the tour party appeared to be congregating. She was pretty sure they were almost at capacity now.

On the whole, the bucket listers appeared to be enjoying themselves with lots of laughter emanating from the tables. Some were having heated debates, but seemed friendly enough; a few looked a bit worse for wear and glazed eyes gave away how much alcohol they had consumed; a small number had dozed off. Seeing all these wonderful elderly people reminded Rachel of Lady Marjorie, who at eighty-six years old was as spritely as many in this group. Her last cruise had been with Marjorie when they had toured the Baltic Sea. Marjorie had declined joining her for this trip as the flight would have been too long for her, but was looking forward to joining Rachel and her parents in the Caribbean for a Christmas cruise later in the year.

Loud clapping pulled Rachel from her happy reverie and she was glad when Prudence rejoined them so that she could hear what Patty had to say. They all turned expectantly towards their latest guest, but Patty now looked confused as to why they were staring at her.

"Well?" asked Charles impatiently.

A vacant look appeared on the woman's face. "Well what?"

"She's damn well forgotten," snapped Charles.

Glenis nudged him to be quiet. She spoke gently to the bemused looking woman. "You had something to tell us, Patty dear, about the death of Mrs F, I think."

"Did I? Oh dear, I think I might have, but I'm afraid it's gone."

Charles opened his mouth to say something, but thought better of it when he recognised Patty was close to tears. Whatever he was going to say changed to, "It doesn't matter, Patty, have you eaten yet?"

Patty's eyes lit up again and she appeared to enjoy being the centre of attention once more as her companions spoke kindly to her, although she continued to look slightly bemused with vacant eyes.

"Where are we going again?" she asked Glenis, who took her hand and sighed.

"We are on a cruise holiday, dear. We are visiting different places in Australia and New Zealand." A look of relief came over Glenis's face as another woman from their previous evening's dinner table, the one who resembled a stick insect and was around the same age as Patty, bustled towards the table, face red with anxiety.

"There you are, Patty! I've been looking everywhere for you. I'm so sorry, she disappeared while I was in the Ladies – I told you not to go anywhere." The woman, clearly distraught, sat down and downed the first drink in front of her, which belonged to Prudence.

"It's alright, Emma, Patty just joined us fifteen minutes ago. No harm done," said Victor, whose bushy eyebrows seemed to have grown even more prominent and moved as one unit.

"Did you hear?" Emma was about to help herself to Glenis's drink but the spritely older woman swiped it away and called a waiter over.

"Why don't you get yourself a drink?" said Charles pointedly as the waiter appeared.

"I'll have one of those cocktails," Emma said, pointing towards Joe Flanders's wife who was just being served another drink. "Would you like a drink, Patty? Yes, she'll have a brandy – give the man your card, Patty."

Rachel was not overly impressed with Emma, who now turned towards her. "Who's this then? Don't tell me they offer that sort of service on this cruise ship as well."

Wide-eyed with shock, Rachel watched as the unpleasant woman tittered, the drink she'd just downed clearly taking effect and any anxiety over her companion completely dissolving. Rachel had always been taught to respect her elders, but this was a step too far. An uncomfortable silence had descended.

"I think I'll say goodnight." She picked up her handbag.

"Oh don't go, Rachel. Emma didn't mean it. Take that back at once, Emma," Glenis said sharply. "Rachel is the young woman who helped me yesterday after the incident in the library."

Turning her nose up at Rachel and slurping rudely through the straw of the cocktail that had just arrived, Emma sniffed loudly. "That's what I was going to tell you – they've arrested that Indian man – the one with the effeminate pink turban."

"That turban represents spring where he comes from. You need to mind your manners," said Charles in defence of his new friend.

Rachel had had enough. She picked up her handbag, nodded to the others and made her way out of the bar. Even her curiosity wasn't piqued enough to spend another minute with the dreadful Emma.

"Cheek! Surely I don't look anything like that sort of woman," she muttered to herself as she walked briskly through the main atrium and upstairs to deck nine and the sanctuary of her room.

Chapter 13

Sarah was called to see a young male passenger with a wheal to his lower left arm. After satisfying herself it was a localised reaction to an insect bite, she treated him with antihistamines. At last she could lock up the medicines cupboard in the medical centre, and once she had updated the computerised records, she looked at the clock: 11pm.

"Time to get some sleep," she said out loud, but her radio went off again.

"There's a young woman in a bit of a state requesting a visit, she sounds very drunk, sorry." The call handler sounded supportive.

Sarah sighed, frustrated and tired. "Where?"

"7354."

She jotted down the room number. "Thanks, I'll go now."

Her plan was scuppered when Alex called her to help him with a child who needed a boil lancing. "Can't the parent help? I am just on my way to see another passenger."

"Sorry, Sarah, we tried that, but she almost fainted. She's a single mum."

Sarah made her way to deck ten and managed to distract the fractious four-year-old with toys and stories. Once he had settled, she held the child's arm to allow Alex to give a local anaesthetic. Alex worked swiftly, lancing the boil and applying a dressing.

"Is Rafa allergic to penicillin?" he asked.

"I don't know, he's never needed medicine before."

"Is he allergic to anything that you know of?"

"No."

"Right, this is a bottle of children's penicillin. You need to give him four of these spoonfuls four times a day until the bottle is finished. If you notice any reaction at all like a rash or facial swelling, you must stop the medicine and call a doctor straight away. Do you understand?"

Rafa's mum nodded.

"I'd better go, Alex. I got a call out to an anxious drunk," Sarah whispered.

"Do you need me to come with you?"

Sarah was tempted to say yes, but looked into his tired eyes. "No, I should be okay. It sounds like a young woman has drunk too much. You never know, she might be asleep by the time I get there. I've not been called again the whole time I've been here so it can't be urgent."

"Alright, I'll give the first dose here and then go to bed."

Sarah took the lift down three flights to the deck because she was lugging the heavy on-call bag. She checked the room number and knocked on the door lightly, but there was no reply. A louder knock yielded the same result.

"Just as I thought," she murmured. "She has probably fallen asleep." Sarah realised she hadn't been given a name. "Well, I'm here now, so—"

She used her universal swipe key to go inside. The room was pitch black enclosed by the heavy room drapes, and she was about to turn-heel, thinking either the call handler had given her the wrong room number or the person was now in a drunken sleep. As she went to close the door, though, she heard a muffled sound coming from the bathroom as if something had fallen over.

"Hello!" She decided to brave switching the light on – the worst that could happen was that she would get an ear-bashing for waking a passenger.

The bed was ruffled as if it had been slept in, but empty. She quickly took in the scene, noticing that it was one of the balcony cabins that had an adjoining room, then walked back a few steps towards the bathroom and knocked on the door.

"Hello, is anyone in there?"

No reply. She tried the door; it was locked.

"Hello, are you alright in there? I'm a nurse from the medical team. Can I help you?"

Still no reply and all was silent.

Sarah suddenly tensed, her heart racing. She had a bad feeling about this, although logic told her the woman had passed out in a drunken stupor, probably after being sick down the toilet.

"I'm coming in."

She used her card as a screwdriver to unlock the bathroom door from the outside, and with shaking hands, gingerly opened it.

The young woman lying in the bath, fully clothed in a bright turquoise cocktail dress, reminded Sarah of someone she had seen earlier that day. Or was it the day before?

Sarah sprang into action, checking for a carotid pulse, while at the same time calling into her radio for the emergency medical team and security. The woman's mobile phone was on the floor and she felt cold to touch; the water in the bath was deep and tepid.

Sarah pulled the plug as Graham arrived. "There's a pulse but it's weak."

Alex, Bernard and Brigitte arrived next having responded to the code blue.

"Right, team, we need to get this girl out of the bath. She's breathing and has a pulse, but she's unconscious."

The team worked swiftly and lifted the girl, who was a lightweight but difficult to manoeuvre in the confined space. Alex took her under the arms from one end while Bernard lifted her from the bottom. Sarah and Brigitte grabbed as many bath towels as they could find and wrapped them around her as soon as she was out.

They carried her through to the bedroom and laid her on the bed. Sarah opened her emergency bag while Brigitte and Bernard quickly removed the wet clothes and dried the young woman off. Her face was pale, and if there hadn't been a pulse, one would imagine she was dead.

"Try not to touch anything else," instructed Graham. "Just in case."

He listened to the girl's chest and felt her pulse, while Sarah took her blood pressure and oxygen saturation.

"Pulse is thready, bradycardic," Graham said, "and air entry is shallow. What's the story, Sarah?"

"I got a call to visit an anxious woman who sounded drunk, but I was delayed as I went to help Alex. I don't even know her name."

"It's Georgia Flanders," said Bernard. "I checked the name on the door."

They all looked at each other in recognition of the name.

"There's an empty bottle of wine over there and another in the bin," said Brigitte.

"Probably drunk, maybe alcoholic poisoning. Any sign of tablets?"

"No, sir," said Alex.

"Well, in light of what happened to her grandmother, we'd better treat the area as a crime scene until it's proven otherwise."

"That new chief's not going to know what's hit him," said Sarah.

"Speaking of whom—" Bernard was waiting for the security team, propping the door open so that passengers wouldn't be disturbed. He might just as well not have bothered as two minutes after the loud and overbearing chief had entered the room, the door to the adjoining suite opened.

"What's going on? Is Georgie okay?" Joe Flanders headed towards the bed, but was stopped in his tracks by Graham and Sarah.

"I'm afraid she's unconscious," said Graham gently.

"Really? What's happened?"

Chief Heel was red-faced and flustered, but remained his tactless self.

"Is this your doing?" He looked fiercely towards the older man.

"No, of course not. Will someone tell me what's happening here?"

"Attempted suicide, that's what's happened," Heel said brashly. "Silly girl," he muttered under his breath before turning to Graham. "She's all yours, Doctor, I'm going to bed."

Graham gazed after the chief in disbelief before turning to Joe.

"Attempted suicide?" Joe sat down on the bed. "That's hard to imagine, she's not the type."

"We don't know if it is attempted suicide yet, she may have just drunk too much and fainted in the bath. Although I'm afraid there is no type when it comes to suicide, sir," said Graham, recovering himself after Chief Heel's exit.

"Look, I'm not some idiot you're talking to. First my mother, now my daughter. How do you know it isn't attempted murder?"

"We don't." Jason's voice was terse as he entered the room.

"Look, Mr Flanders, right now we need to get your daughter down to the medical centre. Please come down as soon as Security Officer Goodridge has finished here. Bernard, why don't you escort Mr Flanders back to his room?"

Jason followed Bernard through the adjoining door without looking at Sarah.

"Alex, fetch a stretcher, will you? I don't think Miss Flanders will manage in a chair."

While they were waiting for Alex, Sarah retrieved Georgia's mobile phone from the bathroom floor, wearing gloves.

"It's a good job she dropped this or I might not have found her." It wasn't unusual for medical staff to be called out to people who had drunk too much and fallen asleep, or as a drunken prank to a room where guests were sleeping soundly, only to be awakened by a bang at the door from medical staff. Thankfully it was not common, but Sarah had been about to put this down to one of those scenarios before hearing the sound coming from the bathroom.

Chapter 14

It had taken an age to find a mattress for the CSO, as tracking down the hotel manager Heinz Linz was no mean feat. The six-foot-three senior officer stood a couple of inches taller than Jason, his frown making his already weather-worn face look like sandpaper.

"Perhaps you could explain why my housekeeping supervisor has spent the past hour consoling one of my best room stewards?"

Jason was torn between loyalty to his boss, a loyalty he was struggling to feel, and the compassion he felt for the poor woman he'd witnessed being bullied.

"I'm sorry, sir. The chief hasn't slept well since arriving on board so he's probably sharper than usual."

Linz's eyebrows raised to the ceiling as he huffed. "Well, we can't have our new security chief suffering from insomnia, can we?" The snarl betrayed his true feelings.

"It would be better for all concerned if he could get a good night's sleep, sir. He is under a lot of pressure and this ship's bigger than the *Jade Queen* where he's come from."

Jason followed Linz downstairs to the large corridor spanning the length and breadth of the ship below the passenger decks, known to crew as the M1 as it had numerous junctions that ran off it to various parts of the ship. They descended a flight of metallic stairs and entered a gigantean storeroom containing new and old mattresses, bedding, pillows and all manner of other equipment neatly stored in orderly bays. It was like a large warehouse.

"I've never been in here before."

"That's because it's off limits to everyone except housekeeping supervisors and myself." Linz relaxed a little and proudly showed Jason around, explaining where everything was stored, and then led him towards the mattress bay. There were huge containers with old mattresses piled on top of each other. "They will be dropped off in Melbourne for disposal. They go to a recycling plant where they salvage as many of the materials as possible. Some of the mattresses are sent to the third world. Queen Cruises is committed to reducing its carbon footprint."

Jason nodded.

"Now, what sort of mattress does Herr Heel require?" Linz, a German, laughed at his own joke.

Jason slapped himself on the head. "A comfortable one?" He grimaced.

"You don't know, do you?"

"No, sir. I was in the forces, we didn't get much choice in the mattress line. I assumed they're all the same."

"Being in the forces is no excuse for ignorance, young man." Linz shrugged and marched away. He returned moments later with a list of all the different mattresses the cruise ship stocked. "Perhaps you can take this to the chief and get him to choose, or better still, bring him down here. We could make all the mattresses up for him, provide a demonstration, he could test each one before making his choice. After all, we have nothing better to do with our time."

Jason decided that he'd got as far as he was going to get with the chief of hotel management, who was struggling to contain his rage beneath an air of caustic sarcasm. It would be better if he didn't add Heel to this simmering cauldron.

"Give me a minute, sir." Jason radioed the chief and, after an initial bark from his boss, he managed to give him four options. If he'd attempted to go through all of them, Heel was likely to want to come down himself.

"Medium-firm, then," Heel snapped. "Just make sure there are no lumps, Goodridge."

Before Jason had time to respond, Heel had cut him off.

Jason turned to find Linz standing immediately behind him. "Did you catch that?"

"Charm personified, isn't he? There, take that one."

Jason followed the nod of the head to a pile third in line while Linz marched away to a desk and fired up a computer to register the removal. Standing in front of the queen-sized mattress, Jason was tempted to ask Linz for help, but thought better of it. Jason was strong as he kept up his rigorous army training by running and using the gym on board ship before passengers were awake, and he pulled weight training in to keep himself in trim. It wasn't the weight that bothered him, it was the shape!

He hauled the cumbersome item to the ground, still covered in plastic. He'd heard one should air mattresses before use, but decided not to broach that subject with either chief.

"By the way, Officer."

Jason turned from the doorway he'd just reached. "Sir?"

"You'll need to bring the old one down here."

Jason saw the flint-like stare in Linz's eyes and knew that his new boss had made a permanent and potentially malicious enemy. A rivalry had been sparked by Heel's treatment of the poor Filipina housekeeping steward, one that Jason was certain would lead to trouble for the CSO.

"Yes, sir, with pleasure."

Jason had just arrived back at the storeroom after delivering the mattress to his boss's room, pleased to discover Heel wasn't there. He had done a quick mattress change, tearing off the plastic and re-making the bed before lugging the old mattress back down to the storeroom, where he found Linz waiting for him.

"Funny how our own Jack Waverley didn't find the mattress uncomfortable. Perhaps he had other things on his mind – Brenda is a beauty." Heinz cackled loudly as Jason's radio went off, calling him to a code blue.

"Sorry, got to go." He shrugged and pushed the mattress towards Linz, who was still giggling like a schoolgirl. Jason rolled his eyes as he dashed up to deck seven. Why did he have to work with eccentric egotists?

The chief bristled past as Jason turned into the corridor of deck seven.

"Ah, Goodridge. There you are. Where do you think you've been?" Not waiting for a response, Heel barked his orders. "Stupid girl, tried to commit suicide. That ridiculous medical guy thinks she might just have drunk too much or that it might be attempted murder. Really, I don't know how Waverley can work with these people, and that nurse – Bradshaw, I think her name is – watch out for her. She's trouble."

Jason had been finding it difficult to contain his anger at the smear on the well-respected Chief Medical Officer's character, but now he found himself blushing and feeling like he couldn't breathe.

"What do you mean?"

"It wouldn't surprise me if she was up to no good. You can't trust people like her."

The lift doors closed and Heel was gone. Jason realised he was shaking, but wasn't certain if it was anger or fear. He had to find out how the chief knew Sarah, and why she wasn't telling him they had met before. Just when he thought things were going so well – he had to admit he had finally fallen in love again after ten years of having the emotions sucked out of him during his stints in Afghanistan, where he'd witnessed things that he could never speak about, but that still haunted his dreams.

Pulling all his emotions into check, just like he'd done in Kabul, he marched towards the stateroom. Jason followed Joe Flanders and Bernard into the stateroom next door, unable to look at Sarah or Dr Graham Bentley after the vitriol his boss had just poured all over him. Heel couldn't have done more harm if he'd poured acid.

Breathing slowly and deeply to slow his pounding heart, with a forced smile, Jason turned towards Flanders.

"Are you alright?" Bernard asked, but Jason turned away as if he hadn't heard.

"Mr Flanders, I need to ask you some questions and then I'll need to go through your daughter's room, if that's okay?"

"Fine, go ahead, ask."

"Could you tell me where your wife is, sir? It might be better if I speak with both of you."

"Why? She's not Georgie's mother."

"Nevertheless, sir, I need to ask some questions, and rather than repeat myself, I'd like to ask both of you."

What Jason really wanted was to watch for any non-verbal signals between the two of them and stop any collusion in case they did have something to hide. While it seemed perfectly reasonable that the girl had got drunk or attempted suicide following the death of her grandmother, he wasn't going to rule out foul play as quickly as his boss seemed to be doing.

"Sorry, I don't know where she is. We had a row, I came to bed. She's probably entertaining some of the elderly guests who are part of our tour."

Jason doubted that, but didn't have much choice but to continue.

"Was your daughter part of the row?"

"Why does that matter?" Flanders's face reddened, his nostrils flared, and Jason was concerned he might keel over.

"Shall we sit, sir? You've had a shock – would you like a drink?"

"Yes, a brandy – you'll find a bottle over there." Flanders nodded towards the table in the centre of the sitting area. "Have one yourself, if you're allowed on duty."

"Thank you, but I don't drink. I'll have a soda water if I may?"

"Suit yourself."

Jason poured drinks and sat down opposite the man. His mind was now back on the job and he sat back, relaxing. It had the desired effect: Flanders opened his mouth and the words tumbled out.

He'd been angry with his mother for years; she was a controlling woman who wouldn't let him have any say in the business he supposedly managed. She still held the reins in every way. His first wife had hated the old girl and got sick of her; their marriage had been stormy and ended a couple of years in. His second wife and the mother of his daughter was more tolerant, but she too had left two years ago after Mrs Flanders the elder had told her she was a money-grabbing piece of dirt.

"Georgie hated her mother leaving, but Priscilla moved to New Zealand and Georgie works for the business, so what could she do? She stayed. Mother doted on her, but the more she tried to win her over, the more distant Georgie became. She blames – erm blamed her grandmother for her mother leaving, but underneath it all, she worships – worshipped her grandmother. She's like her in many ways – hardnosed in business dealings."

That didn't fit with the story Jason had heard that granddaughter and grandmother didn't get on at all. "Go on," he encouraged.

"Chloe and Georgie don't get on, and now Georgie doesn't have an ally in my mother, they're at loggerheads. Tonight they had another row – one of many – nothing unusual, except that Georgie accused Chloe of killing my mother."

"Why would she do that?"

"Just to goad her, I think. Anyway, then I stepped in and told Georgie to apologise. She wouldn't – stormed out of the room and slammed the door. Chloe told me she was sick to death of my family and needed some air. That's the last I saw of either of them until I heard a commotion coming from Georgie's room. Can I go now? I really need to go and see how my daughter is."

"Yes, of course. If I need to ask you anything else I'll come and see you tomorrow. Are you happy for me to go through next door?"

"Help yourself."

Chapter 15

Rachel slept fitfully after her fraught evening, shocked at the unpleasant encounter with stick insect Emma. Surely Emma had noticed her at the dinner table the previous night, although she had bent Glenis's ear most of the time.

Did she really think I was a paid escort or was she just being nasty for reasons unknown? Neither option endeared the woman to her.

Then there had been the conversation with Jason, who was clearly struggling with managing the situation he found himself in. It was unlikely he would report Heel to Captain Jenson, a pleasant but 'old school' type who wouldn't take too kindly to junior officers being disloyal. On the other hand, Heel really was living up to his name. There was nothing to stop her reporting him for his rudeness alone. If she was an ordinary passenger, as she had been on previous cruises, she wouldn't hesitate, but this time she was a guest speaker for the duration. Although she was employed through an agency, it still blurred the lines with regards to her employment responsibilities.

"One more strike and I won't hesitate, Chief Heel."

The morning run, shower and breakfast in the buffet cleared her head, and she made her way to the gym early. The male receptionist with shiny black cropped hair looked up as she entered. Rachel wore loose white slacks and a pink tracksuit top and carried a USB stick in her pocket.

"Can I help you?"

"I'm Rachel Prince. I was told to come here – I have a ten o'clock self-defence class."

The young man beamed at her, revealing perfect white teeth. He looked like an advert for steroids.

"Hi, Rachel, come with me. You've been allocated one of the activity rooms."

Rachel followed him into a large room with glass windows enclosing the space, apart from two main walls displaying activity posters. The shiny wooden oak-effect floor was perfect for fitness activities. Twenty chairs had been set out in a semi-circle with a table at the front. A screen was already raised behind the table and a projector and laptop were available to one side.

"Mats are in there. I wasn't sure if you'd need them for the first session." He nodded towards a cupboard door which she assumed housed other gym equipment too.

"Thank you, I'll see how it goes. We'll help ourselves if we do. Is there a list?"

"Oh yes, sorry, I forgot. I'm pretty new to ship life, not quite in a routine yet. I'm Dan, by the way. I'll go get it for you."

"Thanks, Dan."

Rachel inserted her USB stick into the laptop and checked the projector was working. All good – now all she had to do was deliver. The list didn't arrive until the class was almost full. Rachel assumed Dan had been distracted by guests and class attendees.

"Rachel! We didn't know you were the self-defence trainer," Glenis called out as she entered the room with half a dozen bucket listers, including all those from dinner apart from Deep.

Rachel waved but didn't join them, not wanting to engage in conversation with the stick-insect woman, Emma. She was still annoyed with Emma for implying she was a paid escort at best, a hooker at worst. She checked through the list when Dan finally gave it to her and familiarised herself with names and ages before starting the class.

"Good morning, everyone, I'm Rachel Prince, course leader for the self-defence classes." After introducing herself, explaining her training as a black belt in karate and finding out a little about the class of twenty, including any medical conditions or current injuries, she started.

Following a slow start, the predominantly female class soon gelled. Rachel found it hard to pitch the class to suit the vastly wide age differences, but the bucket listers, along with a small number of people in their sixties and seven women in their twenties, seemed to revel in their inexperience and weren't afraid to mix. Charles was there, a little surprisingly considering his military background, but she suspected he might want to impress the ladies – one in particular as he and Prudence were behaving like giggly teenagers.

The man she'd been introduced to the previous evening, Victor, was also there. Rachel suspected he too had a soft spot for Prudence Crowther, who was very attractive and seemingly happy to flirt. Even Emma and Patty joined in the fun and participated in the practical with extraordinary vigour considering the number of wobbles emanating from an overly tight short skirt and vest, both revealing far too much flesh for Rachel's liking. Emma didn't acknowledge Rachel and didn't appear to recognise her. Neither did Patty, come to think of it.

After class, Glenis frog-marched Emma like a naughty schoolgirl across the room to Rachel while she packed away the laptop to give back to Dan.

"Go on," she cajoled.

Up close, Rachel noticed the vascular lines in the other woman's cheeks: a sure sign of overindulgence of alcohol. Emma avoided eye contact, but muttered reluctantly, "Apparently I owe you an apology."

Rachel waited for the actual apology to come, but it didn't. Emma turned on her heels and strode out the room, leaving Rachel and Glenis stranded. Not liking Emma any more than she had done before, Rachel was at a loss to imagine what was wrong with her.

"Oh dear, I'm sorry, Rachel. I thought she was going to show some regret after insulting you last night, but obviously not." Continuing without waiting for an answer, Glenis spoke in a lowered voice. "When I confronted her this morning, she seemed genuinely surprised, said she didn't have a clue what I was talking about and couldn't believe she would have said such a thing. I don't know her very well at all, but I think she has a lot on her plate looking after Patty, who has memory problems. Dementia, I think."

"Don't worry about it, it was nothing. As you say, perhaps she's under a lot of strain, and she did seem to wallop the alcohol down. Maybe she genuinely doesn't remember."

Glenis looked sceptical. "That's very forgiving of you, but please don't let it stop you meeting us again. Will you join us for dinner this evening? You remind me so much of my granddaughter, and it's nice to have young blood around with us old biddies! I much prefer younger company, but none of my family would come with me on this cruise. My son suggested the bucket list tour when he saw it advertised in the *Times*. He was joking with me as I've never been abroad, except for a trip to Scotland."

Rachel almost spluttered on the glass of water she'd picked up, finding it hard to imagine Scotland being seen as going abroad.

"But you came anyway."

"I was so cross with the family for not taking me seriously when I said I wanted to do something different for a change. I called a friend who knew about the internet and we sat down together while she booked it all for me. My son rued the day he'd shown me the ad when I announced the rest of his inheritance might go on future cruises if I enjoyed this one."

"Did your friend not want to come with you?"

"Sadly, she couldn't afford it – she tries to live on a pittance of a pension after her husband was scammed out of his life savings. The experience drove him to his grave and now she's left with nothing. I try to help when I can."

"How dreadful! Was the scammer caught?"

"Oh yes, he was caught alright, but they hardly got anything back. He'd blown theirs and a number of other people's savings."

"And are you enjoying the cruise, apart from the death of Mrs Flanders of course?"

"I am for the most part, but I do miss my family. Thankfully Prudence appears to be in the same boat so she keeps me company, and Charles has attached himself to us, insisting he will be our protector in case a murderer is lurking in the background. Please come tonight, Rachel."

Rachel had wanted to avoid the main dining room for fear of running into Robert, but she melted at the earnestness in Glenis's grey eyes, visible through the clear lenses of her oversized spectacles.

"It's a date," she conceded as Prudence appeared in the doorway.

"There you are, Glenis. I saw Emma leave in a bit of a huff and wondered if you were alright. Are you coming for lunch?"

Rachel squeezed Glenis's hand and nodded understanding as the woman left to join her friend.

Sarah was already in the buffet along with Bernard and Gwen when Rachel arrived.

"Where's Brigitte and the docs?" she asked as she joined them with a tray laden with fresh salad.

"She's on call, gone to see a bloke with a rash," replied Gwen.

"And Graham wouldn't be seen dead in here," said Bernard, winking at Rachel. "He's probably having a three course lunch in the officers' dining room or giving an account of the events of last night to the captain."

"What events?"

"Keep it down," said Gwen, looking around to check they were not within hearing distance of other passengers. They were all eating late so the buffet was relatively quiet and their table in the corner was well shielded.

"I was called to Georgia Flanders's room last night. She was unconscious in the bath." Sarah's eyes darted around their surroundings. "We thought she was drunk or had taken an overdose, but she says she was drugged."

"Was she?"

"I think so. We have a blood sample to hand in at Burnie tomorrow, but from what she says, it does sound like it."

"Either that or she has an active imagination," interjected Gwen.

"What does the security chief say?"

Sarah's raised eyebrows said it all. "He won't hear of it – says she's a silly girl who tried to commit suicide. Graham tried speaking with him, but he's been unreceptive."

Sarah's eyes filled up.

"What's the matter?"

Bernard shook his head, and as Sarah wiped her eyes on a napkin, the Filipino nurse lay a hand on her shoulder.

"It's Jason, he's been a bit off with Sarah," he explained. "I've told her it's probably working with that man that's driving him to distraction."

"He won't speak to me, Rachel. Last night, I called him after I got to my room and he was gruff, told me he was busy and put the phone down. He's never been like this, ever since I've known him." Sarah's bottom lip trembled and she chewed it mercilessly, as was her habit when worried.

"I met him last night, and he was certainly struggling with his new boss." All eyes were now on Rachel. "Look, there's no excuse for him being standoffish with you, but that man Heel is enough to make the most placid person rage. Jason witnessed his boss giving hell to my room steward over his mattress – something that had nothing to do with her. I found her in tears after the security chief nearly knocked me over while he was storming away and then yelled at me as if it was my fault he'd bumped into me! Jason and I chatted for a while afterwards and he was torn between loyalty to his boss and reporting what he'd witnessed. I can see how that would upset him – perhaps he needs some space to work things out."

"Oh Rachel, that must be it – Jason is loyal through to his bones. This sort of situation would eat at him, that's for sure. I thought maybe Heel had told him he couldn't see me anymore, or worse, he'd got fed up with me."

"You can forget the second part of that sentence," said Gwen. "That man's got it bad, he's besotted with you, Sarah. My advice is give him a bit of space. Anyway, I'd better go and get some billing done or I'll be for it."

After Gwen left, Bernard looked hesitantly at Sarah. "Does Gwen know what happened last night?"

Sarah shook her head, still wiping her eyes.

"What happened?" Rachel noticed the exchanged looks.

"Chief Heel muttered something to Sarah. None of us heard it, but I saw the malice in his eyes as he moved away."

Rachel took Sarah's hand, causing her to look up from her tissue.

"He said he'd make me pay or some such thing – I was concerned for Georgia Flanders so wasn't really listening. It was only afterwards I realised what he had said – but I don't understand it. As far as I know, I've never met him before. He's the strangest man, I'm sure I'd remember if I had."

Concern for her friend welled up in Rachel's chest, along with fear that the new chief of security might actually be dangerous.

"Who has access to personnel files?"

"Each chief officer can access their own team's files, but if you're thinking about Heel's, forget it – only the captain would be able to access them. Or Waverley, but he's sunning himself in the Caribbean."

"I don't suppose he's let Deep go yet?"

"Yes he has, this morning. Sorry, I forgot to tell you. Graham had results back from Adelaide's coroner: the snake had had its venom removed so was not dangerous.

Mrs F was poisoned by a neurotoxin that paralysed and killed her, they are still running toxicology tests. Heel was ordered by the captain to let the man go unless he had any evidence to charge him. Apparently he's been in high dudgeon ever since and won't speak to Graham, as if it's his fault the snakebite didn't kill her."

"They found a snake box in Mr Janda's room so the snake could still have been his," Bernard added.

"So the murder was elaborately staged – presumably the murderer was going to remove the snake after it had bitten Mrs F and let everyone think she had been stabbed to death or killed by a venomous snake that wouldn't be found. I can't believe the snake was Deep's, perhaps someone planned to frame him or they planted the box on spec after he disturbed them in the library."

"That's what it looks like," Bernard sighed. "We need you more than ever, Rachel. The CSO is unhinged, and even if he does investigate, he won't unearth the real killer. He goes around like a bull and doesn't have the intelligence to investigate a wily murderer such as this one."

"And apparently he's still convinced that Mr Janda committed the murder, by all accounts." Sarah looked pleadingly at Rachel.

"You and I need to take that look in Mrs F's room tonight after all."

Sarah blew her nose, looked up and stuck her chin out. "You're on."

"Not without me, you're not. What can I do?" asked
Bernard.

Chapter 16

Rachel had forgotten it was a formal evening where passengers met the captain and his crew until Sarah called to say she'd see her there. After frantically rushing to change into a graduated grey evening gown, pulling on coral sandals, a coral shrug, and placing her door card in a small coral handbag, she barely had time to apply any makeup, let alone brush through her long blonde mane.

Standing at an inch under six feet and used to keeping herself in shape, she looked in the mirror and was pleased with her appearance. Her bright blue eyes stared back at her – Carlos would approve. Appreciative glances from passers-by confirmed she had done a decent job of dress and makeup as she made her way downstairs to join the throngs of people gathering in the main atrium.

Rachel was soon joined by Charles, quickly followed by Prudence, Glenis and the forgetful Patty, but she was pleased to see that Emma was not with them.

Glenis spoke first as she took Rachel's arm. "Good evening, Rachel, I told the others you would be joining us for dinner, and they were so pleased. Isn't this exciting?"

"It would be if the waiters would be a bit more generous with the champers," complained Charles.

Prudence nudged him as a waiter stood directly behind him. "Drinks, ladies?" The waiter skirted round Charles to offer the women champagne. "Sorry, sir, none left." His smirk suggested he'd heard Charles's comment.

"I suppose I deserved that," Charles responded good-naturedly, but not to be outdone, he reached out and grabbed a flute from another passing waiter's tray.

"What are we doing here again? And where's Emma?" asked Patty.

"I'm here, Patty? Remember, we talked about this, I have to do things alone sometimes."

Emma had appeared from nowhere and somehow managed to shove enough people out of the way to join the group. The woman wore a bright red evening dress and would have been good looking if she added a little more weight. The spider veins had been covered with concealer, although the inability to smile revealed what Rachel imagined were many years of Botox as well as her nasty side.

Patty was dressed in a revealing evening gown that must have required assistance to get over the bulges. Charles's eyes were firmly drawn to Patty's bosoms dancing up and down as she struggled for breath beneath the tight-fitting gown.

"Sorry," she finally said quietly.

Hubbub from too many passengers squeezing into the spaces in and around the large atrium and extending on to and up the stairs to the next deck that circled the area made it difficult to hear any further conversation. Rachel was relieved to see her escape route as the medical team arrived, dressed in their formal evening whites that somehow outshone their usual dazzling whites.

"I've just seen a friend, I'll see you at dinner." Rachel prised her arm away from Glenis's grasp and gave the woman a kiss on the cheek.

"I see you've made some friends," Brigitte remarked with a roll of the eyes as Rachel joined the medics.

"They're a nice bunch," answered Rachel, not mentioning the not-so-nice Emma.

"Who's the one who put the dress on and missed?" asked the incorrigible Bernard.

"I don't know her well, but her name's Patty. You all look wonderfully smart, by the way. You make me feel underdressed."

"As always you look like you just came off the catwalk, Rachel Prince. If the captain wasn't so close I'd give you a wolf whistle."

"And you'd get a slap for your trouble, Bernard. Behave." Gwen scolded him, but the twinkle in her eye gave her away.

"Miss Prince, good to see you again." Captain Jenson stopped to shake her hand. "I understand you've met our new chief of security, Chief Heel."

Was that the hint of humorous light dancing in the captain's eyes or had he too tasted the champagne?

"Miss Prince has been helpful to us on a few occasions, Heel. You'd do well to liaise with her if you can't get our little business sorted out soon." Any sense of a smile departed from the captain's face and a warning shot replaced it.

Heel spluttered, and with a face like thunder replied, "Ha, ha, Captain. Very funny, involve a passenger in security business. I see you have a quick wit." The empty laugh from Heel fell on deaf ears as the captain had already moved on, followed by Rachel and the medical team.

Rachel almost felt sorry for the irritating man, but her heart hardened as she remembered he had threatened her best friend. Certain the man had caused the rift between Jason and Sarah, Rachel determined to track Jason down to find out what was going on. For now she was satisfied that Captain Jenson appeared to be on to the chief of security, but the veiled warning was unlikely to have any impact on the strange man.

Sarah and the medical team watched on as the captain introduced his senior officers and spoke highly of his Chief Medical Officer, Dr Graham Bentley. Signs of Sarah chewing her bottom lip signalled that she was still concerned about something.

Jason most likely, although it could be concern about the threat from Heel.

After the ceremony and formal introductions were over, Rachel signalled to Sarah that they were still on for a visit to Mrs F's room in the early hours. They had agreed to meet at 4am when even the most die-hard passengers should be in bed, and the housekeeping staff wouldn't be due to start work for a while. Breathing in a deep sigh, she headed towards the Coral Restaurant.

The first person she saw as she walked towards the table was Deep. Thrilled to see the man who had confided in her about his previous relationship with Florence Flanders, she bent down and kissed him on the cheek.

"I'm so pleased to see you. I was worried."

Deep's eyes were grief stricken and the lines on his face appeared deeper. "Thank you, Rachel. It was a misunderstanding. I would never have harmed Florence. No matter what you hear over the coming days, please believe that."

Rachel took her seat next to him, confused, but didn't get the opportunity to ask any more as Glenis was keen to monopolise her as her invited guest.

"I'm so pleased you could join us again, Rachel. Isn't it good to have Deep back with us? Wasn't the captain charming? He spoke to us, you know. You should have stayed with us, I could have introduced you."

Rachel was wondering where the timid Glenis of two days ago had disappeared to and beginning to understand that perhaps she wasn't as unassuming as she made out.

A good reader of people, Rachel wondered if the 'almost faint' had been an attention seeking ruse, but chastised herself for being unkind. Glenis had admitted to being lonely earlier.

"I think I saw the captain speaking with Rachel so I don't think she missed out. Well, you wouldn't, would you, when you're as beautiful as she is?" Charles winked admiringly towards Rachel.

"Oh but—"

"They looked quite pally, if you ask me," Charles continued, cutting off Glenis in her prime.

"I was with my friend who's a nurse on board, she introduced me." Rachel didn't want to give too much away in case any of the people assembled had anything to do with the murder. They all seemed to have got over it very quickly and none of them showed any signs of sorrow, apart from Deep.

"Did you hear, that daughter of Joe Flanders tried to commit suicide?" Rachel noticed Patty and Emma at the opposite side of the table. It was Emma who spoke.

"Nooooo!" said Prudence.

"Yes, Joe was telling me earlier. Seems she might have taken an overdose."

Why would Joe Flanders say that about his own daughter when he would have been informed by Dr Bentley that he didn't believe this was the case? Surely his daughter would have told him she thought she was drugged? What an odd family.

"Why would she do that?" asked Deep, concerned.

Emma huffed, but was clearly pleased to be centre of attention. "I don't know. The whole family's bonkers if you ask me. First the mother, now the daughter."

"Mrs Flanders hardly brought about her own demise." Deep raised his voice. "You should show some respect, Mrs Grant."

"Well I never—"

Glenis intervened. "Yes, let's forget about these unfortunate goings on. I'd much rather talk about the captain and his crew. The champagne was magnificent."

"Yes, and you imbibed a little too much of it, Glenis dear," said Prudence.

That would account for the rather loose tongue, thought Rachel as she quietly observed this group of elderly people thrown together by their bucket list tour. It would be interesting to find out why exactly each one had opted for the cruise and whether any of them knew Mrs Flanders before sailing, and if they did, why were they not saying as much? Rachel noticed Patty's eyes quickly moving from glaring at Deep to bemused.

Emma continued to hold court throughout the meal, and although caustic, she was mildly amusing. There didn't appear to be any other endearing qualities about her, and she was so loud, people at other tables would occasionally look up, irritated.

Robert's table was empty and Rachel found herself wondering where he was.

"I see you're wondering where your old friend is this evening." Deep pulled her attention back from the past.

"Guilty as charged. I don't know why as I don't really want to know. I'm pleased he's not here tonight."

"Are you sure? I recognise that look, Rachel, I've felt the same myself for many years. Don't go back, you should always go forwards in life. Look what happens when you go back." Deep opened out the palm of his hand as he spoke.

"You're right, but I don't want to go back. I'm engaged."

"In that case, I'm delighted for you. May I see the ring?"

Rachel held up her left hand, inadvertently drawing the attention of the others away from Emma and Patty, who both gave her daggers.

"It's beautiful, Rachel. You weren't wearing a ring the day we boarded, though, I would have noticed," remarked Glenis.

"So would I," said Charles, clearly not averse to a little flirtation even with a woman decades younger than himself.

"I wasn't, you're right. I only got engaged a few days before the cruise and I hadn't told my best friend. I wanted to share the news with her in person."

"More likely, didn't want the men to know," she heard Emma whisper loudly to Patty. None of the others appeared to hear, or they pretended not to, so Rachel did the same.

"Well congratulations," said Glenis, calling the drinks waiter over. "Champagne all round, please, we're celebrating. Put it on my tab."

"Yes, congratulations," said Emma, obviously not wanting to miss out on a drink that someone else was paying for.

The group was engaged in loud conversation over dinner after the champagne had taken effect, so Rachel turned to Deep.

"I notice you're not drinking much?"

"Nor you, I see. Perhaps neither of us is cut out for excess."

"Perhaps not, but the others are enjoying themselves and I don't begrudge them. May I ask what happened to you after you left with the chief of security last night?"

"Shall we go somewhere quieter after dinner and I'll explain?"

Rachel had no trouble escaping Glenis's attentions as Prudence and Charles suggested she might need an early night as she could barely stand. They supported her with assistance from Victor, who'd joined them for dessert. Emma and Patty disappeared as soon as the dessert menu was handed out and coffee was ordered, or more realistically as soon as the drink had run out. Patty seemed to move in and out of awareness, at times forgetting where she was and at others seemingly fully aware of who was who around the table.

"Would you be truly offended if I asked you to accompany me to the cigar lounge?" Deep asked sheepishly.

Rachel laughed. "Not at all, I'm exposed to a lot worse than cigar smoke in cop land."

"I would be very interested to hear about your work. Are you, by any chance, secretly investigating Florence's murder?"

"Let's put it this way, I would like to know who killed your friend, if only to remove suspicion from you."

"And how do you know I didn't do it?"

"I don't for certain, but for now, I trust my instincts. Something is going on, and for some reason I believe you are being framed. What I don't know yet is whether the killer was after Mrs Flanders or whether he or she is after you. That's why I need your help."

Deep's eyes darted back and forth for a brief moment, digesting the information.

They arrived at the cigar bar and found a small table in a corner. A pianist was playing the baby grand piano, and the smoke-filled air irritated Rachel's eyes for a moment until they adjusted. While she preferred smoke-free areas, she was used to entering houses and establishments where the term smoke-free was unheard of, the latest being the premises of an illegal hock-making ring. Every bust she had been involved in featured rooms barely visible through the smoke, with no windows to let the outside world know what was taking place inside the walls of the makeshift buildings. The hock was so strong it had been poisoning people, which brought it to the attention of the Met, and she had been on one of the many teams of police officers involved in dawn raids of multiple premises simultaneously. The gang leaders were arrested and their shady business brought to a close, but Rachel was well aware that the next gang would be waiting in the wings to take over. Her job consisted of cutting off tentacles, only for more to appear, but she still loved arresting bad guys.

"What would you like to drink, Rachel?"

"Martini and lemonade, please."

Deep called a waiter over. "Martini and lemonade for the lady and port for me." He looked at Rachel. "One of the many habits I acquired during my time in England: an after-dinner cigar with a glass of port or brandy."

"How very *Downton Abbey*," Rachel teased.

"Indeed, I watched that series on Netflix – wonderful. I'm pleased you're looking into this matter, Rachel, but whatever is going on, I don't want you to put yourself in danger on my account. Promise me you will be careful."

"I promise."

"Okay, Chief Security Officer Heel first of all took me to his rather grand office and questioned me extensively about the events in the library on embarkation day – it seems a lifetime ago, doesn't it? Anyway, at first he was brusque but pleasant, but when I just repeated what I had already told him, all sense of pleasantry left and he as much as accused me of planting a snake in the library. I told him that was preposterous, I knew nothing about snakes and had done no such thing. I didn't even know a snake had been involved or I might have managed to get an anti-venom in time to treat poor Florence."

Deep put his head in his hands for a moment as the drinks arrived. He looked up again and inserted the cigar into his mouth, exhaling the smoke before continuing.

"He showed me a glass case that I had never seen before and told me it had been found in my room. I was astonished, but the chief grinned as if he'd caught me out, asked me to explain that away if I could. Of course, I couldn't because I didn't know what it was or what significance it had."

"Do you have any idea who could have put it there?"

"My roommate is the only person with a key card, but I can't imagine him doing so. The poor man was banned from our room when they put me under house arrest and had to share with Charles who had a room to himself. He slept on his bed settee for the night. The next thing I knew, another man from the bucket list tour party, a Sir Edward Reynolds – a retired barrister, as it happens, went to see the captain and I was released."

"They didn't say anything else?"

"No, what else is there? Do you know something I don't? I've yet to thank this Sir Edward, I only met him briefly when we stayed in a hotel the night before we left. He keeps himself to himself as far as I can find out. I don't even think I was meant to know about him, but that man Heel couldn't help calling him an interfering old fool who should keep out of his way. He wasn't any more complimentary about the captain. I even heard him railing at one of the security guards about the chief medical officer and, I'm afraid, a nurse – I hope it wasn't your friend?"

Rachel's heart skipped a beat and anger caused her to momentarily lose composure, but she quickly recovered, picked up her drink and smiled at Deep.

"I wouldn't have thought so, they don't know each other."

"Is your friend the nurse who spoke with me after Florence died, Nurse Bradshaw? She was so kind."

"Yes, that's her, and yes, she is kind."

"I don't know what's wrong with that security chief, but it seems to me he's a bomb waiting to explode. I met people like him in the army, post-traumatic-stress-disorder I think they call it these days. Men either go into themselves or become detonators. I fear he's the latter – wouldn't surprise me if he's ex-forces."

That made sense. Perhaps they were dealing with someone who was mentally ill in the new chief. She still needed to find out what he had against Sarah and it didn't excuse his abrasive behaviour, but it could explain it.

"I think you might be right on that score. Are you likely to see him again?"

"Oh yes, I have to report daily. He told me I was out on bail, laughed in my face as he said it."

"In that case, Deep, it would be helpful if you could get him to open up."

"What makes you think he'll tell me anything?"

"Because he can't help himself. He needs to let the anger out and you are one target, but he has others. You just need to discover the right buttons to press and I'm sure he'll reveal all."

"What if I could have saved her, Rachel?"

"You couldn't have. The snake was not venomous, she was poisoned." That was the best Rachel could say to reassure him without divulging what she had learned.

Deep accepted her verdict quietly and agreed to report any further conversations with Heel. Deciding it was time to get a few hours' sleep before her night-time incursion into Mrs F's room, Rachel bid her new kindly but frail friend goodnight.

Chapter 17

Sarah was already waiting outside the luxury suite at the rear of deck fifteen. This was the suite Marjorie usually stayed in when cruising, so it felt odd sneaking around in the early hours outside a room Rachel would usually have been welcomed into.

"I thought you'd never get here. I've been waiting for ages."

Rachel looked at her watch – 4am was the time they'd agreed, but she decided not to add to her friend's stress levels that were clearly at boiling point.

"Sorry."

Sarah used her medical staff's universal swipe key to open the door. "I'm getting flashbacks of another room search, I'm really not sure we should be doing this."

"We're here now so let's take a quick look inside." Rachel encouraged her friend through the door before putting Sarah's swipe card into the slot for power. "That chief hasn't even screened the room off."

"It feels like raiding a tomb," said Sarah.

"Hardly! I think you're being a bit melodramatic. Come on, the sooner we look, the sooner we can get out of here. Is Bernard on standby?"

"Yes, he's prepared."

"Good." Rachel looked around the suite consisting of lounge, separate bedroom, large bathroom and balcony spanning both of the main rooms. The lounge remained untouched: evidence of Mrs F having had drinks on arrival sat on a large coffee table undisturbed by the butler. If the butler was Mario who she had met previously, he had more sense than the new chief of security and would have made sure no-one disturbed the room. The *Coral News* lay next to the empty glasses, alongside a folder.

Rachel picked up the folder.

"It's the bucket list itinerary. I can't believe Heel hasn't taken this stuff away and examined it for clues." She flicked through the pages while Sarah looked in the bathroom.

"Is there anything in the folder?"

"Not sure, there's the full list of people on the tour with home addresses, likes, dislikes, dietary requirements, allergies, and next of kin details. I think I'd like to take this with me and study it later."

"Two glasses," Sarah remarked.

"Yep, I wonder who she had a drink with before going to meet Deep."

"Her son Joe?"

"No, he was still in the purser's office. Remember? You mentioned it on the first day and Prudence confirmed they were still there when I was with them after the body had been found. I'm amazed it's not been bagged as evidence."

"At least the room's been left as it was."

"I suppose we have to be thankful for small mercies. Is Mario still the butler for these two rooms?"

"Yes, and thanks to you he's now on treatment for his thyroid disease."

"I'll see if I can catch up with him tomorrow, he might know who was in the room with her. Was there anything in the bathroom? Syringe and needle perhaps with fingerprints?" Rachel laughed.

"You wish! A toiletry bag, with all the usual contents, toothbrush and toothpaste neatly laid out on the shelf. A dirty towel – looks like she'd washed but not used the shower or bathtub. That's all."

"Okay, bedroom."

Rachel led the way through the door into the large bedroom. The balcony curtains had been left open, the balcony being dual aspect with sliding doors leading out from either room. The bed was still made up for the first day of a cruise with a large bed protector sitting at the foot and an opened but not unpacked suitcase on top.

"She hadn't unpacked. It's sad, isn't it?" said Sarah.

Rachel didn't feel it was time for melancholy. She lifted clothes out of the suitcase, looking for anything that might be of importance. Once all the clothes were piled onto the bed, she sighed.

"Nothing, this is hopeless. She must have had a laptop and personal details. Was there a handbag in the library?"

"Yes, Heel did take that away. He may have given it back to Joe."

"Does Joe or his family have access to this room?"

"I don't think so. Normally I would ask Jason, but—"

Rachel sat next to Sarah on the bed and put her arm around her. "Everything will be fine between you and Jason. He'll come to his senses." Struck by inspiration, Rachel got up quickly. "The safe! She's probably put the laptop in the safe like I do."

Sarah followed her through to the lounge. Rachel bent down to open a cupboard, where inside lay the safe.

"It's locked so she has put something in there."

"Try 1, 2, 3, 4," said Sarah.

The safe didn't open, so Rachel pressed the 'clear' button. "It'll be her date of birth or some combination of that, I'm sure."

"That's 11 December 1937."

"How on earth did you remember that, Nurse Bradshaw?" Rachel's mouth opened.

"I've always been good with dates. I had to fill out the paperwork for the death notice before Graham signed it. I remember thinking her birthday was two weeks before Christmas and she was born two years before the Second World War. It must have stuck."

Rachel tapped in 1112 and the door clicked open. She kissed her friend on the cheek.

"You're a genius."

"Never in any doubt." Sarah grinned. "But get on with it, I don't like being here."

Rachel pulled a small, soft leather briefcase out of the safe. "I think it will be better if we take these back to my room and return them tonight. You're right, we should go."

"Hello, Chief, how are you this fine morning?" Bernard's voice screeched through Sarah's radio. She and Bernard had left their radio mics open on a secure channel between them so he could warn her if anyone approached.

"What's it to you?" they heard the chief snarl.

Rachel raced back into the bedroom and returned the clothes to the suitcase. Sarah checked the spy hole into the corridor.

They heard Bernard, undeterred, stalling for time. "Chief, I need to ask you something personal."

"What is it? I'm in a hurry."

Rachel and Sarah dived out the door, taking the back corridor to the opposite side of the deck before Sarah gave her coded message.

"Bernard, I need you in the treatment room."

"On my way," came the reply. "I'll catch you later, Chief."

Rachel couldn't help grinning as they made their way back to the central lifts where they met Bernard.

He smirked. "Didn't I do well?"

"Yes, but a bit too close for comfort, if you ask me. Come on, we're going to Rachel's room."

The relieved trio arrived in Rachel's room. It was still before dawn, but Rachel opened the drapes. "Coffee first and then we can take a look at the loot."

"For a police officer, you're sailing a bit too close to the wind," Sarah chastised her friend.

Just as they'd sat down, there was a loud knock at the door. They looked at each other and Rachel placed the briefcase and folder under the bed. She looked through the spy hole.

"It's Jason," she hissed. "Look natural."

"At five o'clock in the morning, like that's going to work," said Bernard.

Rachel opened the door. "Jason, hello. What can I do for you?"

"May I come in?"

"Erm, well, we were just having an early morning drink before Sarah and Bernard go to work, but yes, do come in."

Jason's furrowed brow and his stern look were unmistakeable as she opened the door to allow him into the room.

"Would you like a coffee?"

"You can cut the pretence." He marched over to the coffee table and sat in one of the chairs opposite Sarah and Bernard.

"What do you mean?" asked Sarah. "And why have you been ignoring my calls?"

"You left this behind." He dropped Sarah's swipe key on to the table and laughed loudly.

"I forgot to mention Jason was with the Chief when I stalled them." Bernard looked apologetically towards Jason.

"I wondered what you were doing lurking around the lifts at that time in the morning, no emergency bag in tow. Then, when I entered Mrs Flanders's room, the lights were on. I saw the swipe card in the slot."

"Did Heel notice?" asked Rachel.

"No, he was slower than me so assumed I'd put my card in. He's easily fooled and didn't want to be there anyway. I'd persuaded him to take a look, partly to distract him when he called me in the early hours to moan he hadn't slept because his pillows were hard! First it was the mattress, now the pillows. Anyway as he hadn't ordered a search after immediately jumping to the conclusion that the woman had been murdered by Manandeep Janda, I thought it would save me another ear bashing. Funnily enough, we didn't find anything. The safe was empty. He yelled at me for wasting his time and headed back to bed, but not before ordering me to find him some new pillows before tonight." Jason sighed deeply. "So, come on, time to tell me what you found."

Rachel poured Jason a coffee before pulling out the briefcase and folder from under the bed. "We haven't had a chance to look at this lot yet, we were going to return it tonight."

Jason frowned. "I hope there isn't anything because I'm going to have a difficult job telling Heel where I got these if there is. Look, I need to go and take over from the night security guys, I'll collect them from you later, Rachel. Let me know if you find anything. Sarah, can I have a word?"

As Sarah followed Jason into the corridor, Rachel read through the contents of the folder while Bernard sat back and enjoyed his coffee. After he had finished, he got up.

"Sorry, Rachel. I'd better go and get washed and changed before I collect the on-call bag from Gwen. I'm on call until tonight. I'm no good at detective work anyway. Good luck."

She smiled. "Thanks, Bernard, you're superb at subterfuge, though."

Sarah came back in as Bernard left. Rachel looked up from the papers.

"He seems to think I'm hiding something from him, he repeatedly asked where I know Chief Heel from." Throwing her hands in the air, Sarah flopped onto the settee. "I told him I don't know the man from Adam, and if I've ever met him it must have been through work."

"Rack your brains, Sarah, because if you do know that man, you need to find out why he's got it in for you and why he's threatened you. Maybe a relative died or something and he blames you."

Sarah crumpled. "Don't you think I've tried, Rachel? Don't you start – I do not know him. I'm sure I'd remember if I had met him, he's unforgettable. I don't know why he dislikes me so much. His malevolence frightens me, I'm not used to being threatened. I know you come across this all the time in your job, but apart from the odd psychotic, confused or drunk patient, it's not my bag. I can cope with anything when I'm in the treatment centre or the infirmary, but a chief of security with a grudge that has my name on it is a new one on me."

Tears flowed and Rachel hugged her.

"If you say you don't know the man, that's good enough for me, and it should be good enough for Jason."

"I think he's trying to believe me, but he's not big on trust. He had a fiancée who went off with another man while he was on tour in Afghanistan. After that he threw himself into work, apparently even put himself in the firing line a couple of times. He's lucky he's still alive, but many of his friends aren't and sometimes these things eat away at him. The thing is, he's only just started opening up to me, and now he doesn't know whether to trust me. He's hurting, Rachel."

"I didn't realise, and I'm sorry, but he should know you better than to think you could ever hide anything from anyone close – you're an open book!" Rachel lifted Sarah's chin to look her in the eyes. "He loves you, Sarah. It's clear to see, and he will come round."

Sarah sniffed. "Do you think so?"

"I know so. Look, why don't we snatch an hour's sleep before going on land? I can look at this stuff tonight. I'll take the bed-settee, you take the bed."

Sarah yawned loudly. "I think sleep would help." She headed to the bed, climbed under the covers and was out like a light.

If only I could sleep like a nurse, Rachel thought as she continued to flick through the papers in her hand.

Chapter 18

Rachel gently tapped on Sarah's shoulder. "Wake up, sleepyhead, remember we're heading out early today."

Sarah lifted a tousled head of light-brown wavy hair from under the covers and looked at Rachel through slit eyes.

"What time is it?"

"Seven o'clock. We docked in Burnie an hour ago. I'm going for a run, see you for breakfast." Sarah had the day off and the two of them were going on a tour to Cradle Mountain with the bus leaving at eight-thirty.

Sarah pulled the covers over her head. "Okay, see you in the buffet at eight."

Rachel pulled the covers back. "Oh no you don't. Come on, sit up, I've made you coffee."

Sarah looked as though she was about to protest, but changed her mind and sat up straight.

"You're right, I'd better get a move on. I'll head back to my room to change after I've finished the coffee. See you in forty-five."

This time Rachel believed her so headed upstairs for her morning run. Port activity had already begun with large container ships emptying their heavy loads. The noise of machinery and shouting spoiled an otherwise beautiful sun-kissed morning.

A few early-bird passengers were already up and about, and she passed a number of people she recognised from the bucket list tour, noticing others from the party power-walking around the deck below.

No wonder they look so well, they're fitter than a lot of my colleagues. Rachel thought of the desk sergeant, a portly man who couldn't have been older than mid-forties, but who could barely lift himself out of his chair. Age is all in the mind, her father often told her. In his Hertfordshire parish, he had a group of elderly men and women in his congregation who'd formed a local ramblers' group and put many of their younger counterparts to shame.

After running for twenty minutes, Rachel returned to her room. Sarah had already left. She quickly showered and dressed, locking away the laptop and files from the night-time foray in the safe with her own laptop before she made her way up to the buffet to meet Sarah.

They rapidly ate breakfast, returned to their respective rooms to clean their teeth, and then met up again in the Coral Theatre at the bow of the ship. They were given tour badges to wear and directed to follow a group down to the dockside.

"Rachel, oh goody, you're on the same tour as us."

Rachel turned to see Glenis, Prudence, Charles, Victor, Emma and Patty. Patty appeared bemused and Emma glared.

"This is my friend, Sarah. Sarah, this is Glenis."

"Hello, Glenis."

"I'm Charles, this is Victor and this is Prudence," said Charles. Emma and Patty had turned their backs and were talking to a few other bucket listers. "That's Emma and Patty," he whispered. "Emma can be a bit off with people."

Emma turned sullenly. "We've met," she snapped.

Sarah smiled politely. "I've already met a few people," she said, but didn't elaborate.

"Sarah's a nurse on board ship," explained Rachel. "She has to be careful about confidentiality so you won't get another word out of her. Looks like we're being asked to board the coach."

"See you later, Rachel," said Glenis, who for once didn't insist she sit with the bucket listers at the front of the coach. Rachel and Sarah made their way towards the back.

"Sorry, I got to know them after the incident in the library. How did you meet Emma?"

Sarah lowered her voice. "It wasn't her I was called to see, it was Patty, the woman she seems to be in charge of – I would say cares for, but she didn't strike me as that caring at all."

"Patty's the one with memory problems – is it Alzheimer's?"

"Not as far as we're aware. She doesn't seem to have a dementia diagnosis at all, but certainly displays memory problems and the occasional bizarre behaviour. Her friend says she's been like it for the past few months, but insisted they come on this tour. Emma said she can be quite determined at times and believes Patty knows she's losing her mind. I've told her she really should see a doctor when they return home."

"Where's home?"

"Oxfordshire. Emma seems to live off the other woman's wealth. Patty apparently paid for her to accompany her on this trip, and although Emma insists she didn't want to come, she's certainly availing herself of all the facilities – driving the stateroom steward mad with her demands."

Rachel laughed. "I can imagine. You know she accused me of being a paid escort the second time I met her? She doesn't like me at all. Patty does seem vacant at times, and at others she appears totally lucid."

"It can be like that with early dementia."

"I wonder if Emma's after her money."

Sarah didn't respond to Rachel's remark, instead saying,. "Oh no, put your head down, Rachel. Another group has just boarded the coach."

A feeling of dread filled Rachel and her heart dropped into her stomach.

"Robert?"

"Yes, they've sat down about four rows ahead. They've not seen us so don't worry."

"Curse that man! I'd just about forgotten he was on board – why is he here? It seems too much of a coincidence to me that we should end up on the same cruise on the opposite side of the world."

The coach started its journey before Rachel got the opportunity to jump off. The familiar sound of a tour guide speaking into a microphone from the front of the bus distracted her for a short time and she looked out the window. The journey was going to take an hour and a half, so she had plenty of time to come up with a strategy to avoid her ex.

An inner voice questioned whether she really was over him, but as she twirled the engagement ring on her left ring finger and Carlos's face filled her mind, the answer to that question was easy. Robert's presence disturbed her, but not because she was still in love with him; rather it was something Deep had said about men like Robert liking the chase. It sent cold shivers down her spine.

"Are you alright, Rachel?" Sarah asked as the guide stopped speaking for a short time.

"Yes, annoyed he's here, but I'm not going to let him ruin our day out."

"You look tired. I was going to ask you if you found anything among those papers, but I think you should sleep for a while if you can."

"You're right." Rachel's eyes felt heavy through lack of sleep and were stinging. She resisted the urge to fight it and closed the heavy eyelids, drifting into a deep slumber.

The coach engine switching off caused Rachel to jump and for a few moments she forgot where she was. Sarah's reassuring hand on her arm reminded her.

"You were out for the count. Stay still a minute, I'll let you know when scumbag and crew have got off."

They waited a few minutes until most people were off the coach. As Rachel stood up, she saw Robert's group at the edge of the crowd, engrossed in what seemed to be a heated debate. The Asian woman was wearing Western clothes today, and Rachel noticed her and Robert occasionally touching each other's backs and arms, intimately but surreptitiously.

"I think they're on a work do of some sort."

"What makes you think that?" asked Sarah.

"They're watching that couple over there. I noticed the couple on the beach on Kangaroo Island before Robert and his party moved off, and look how one of them is constantly watching them."

"Oh, well that's a good thing because it means it's a coincidence you're on the same ship. Robert won't be looking out for you." Sarah sounded happy as they stepped down from the coach.

"And it looks like he's having a fling with one of the team, who I'm sure is married to that guy over there."

"OMG, Rachel. Is that the Asian woman? Do you think her husband is that tall guy with the black beard and moustache?"

Rachel nodded as she looked at the other man. Burly, around six-foot tall, he appeared to be mixed-race Asian and British. He was engrossed in conversation with the other man and women in the party, seemingly oblivious to the chemistry that was oozing between his wife and Robert.

"He really is a scumbag. He's obviously been promoted – detective inspector, I would think, because the others are at his beck and call. I'll put money on the fact he did marry and his wife's back home, oblivious just like I was." An angry tear fell from Rachel's eye and she quickly wiped it away.

"As I said before, you had a lucky escape. I wonder who the couple are and why they would be followed all the way to Australia."

"No idea, but it must be part of some international corruption, maybe money laundering or drugs. Robert's team will be working in partnership with the Australian authorities, I would imagine."

"We're not getting involved with that, are we?"

"If it wasn't Robert and he wasn't behaving like a complete jerk, I'd be interested, but I'm not. Anyway, we've got enough on our plates trying to clear Deep's name and find out why Chief Heel has set his sights on you – not in a good way."

Rachel and Sarah boarded a shuttle bus that would take them to Lake St Clair, ensuring as they got on that they were well away from Robert's group. Once they arrived at the lake, they opted to go for a walk by themselves along a boardwalk. Glenis and the bucket listers stuck with the tour guide and Robert's group disappeared.

"This is beautiful." Sarah took deep, purposeful breaths, taking in the fresh air and relative quiet of the isolated area they now found themselves in. They decided to leave the boardwalk and explore the more rugged surroundings beside the lake after spotting some unfamiliar birdlife and spring flowers. Sarah, a keen photographer, had her camera out in an instant and was snapping madly, taking macro shots of fauna, flowers and bees, and then switching over to snapping photos of birds with her zoom lens. Rachel happily watched her friend utilising the SLR camera she carried everywhere as they walked among reeds. Sarah rarely used her mobile phone to take photos, whereas that's all Rachel used.

"Do you think they have snakes out here?" The sudden memory of the Krait found on board the *Coral Queen* brought Rachel back to the present.

"Oh yes, I forgot, I'm sure they do. I don't think our footwear is suitable for this terrain anyway. Perhaps we should head back to the boardwalk." Sarah swung her camera back round her neck… and then they saw it.

They were arrested in their tracks by a pair of feet sticking out from behind a rock. Rachel stopped to assess for danger as per her police training, but Sarah's nurse training was different and she headed straight around the rock to assist. Satisfied there was no-one else around, Rachel joined her friend, who was already checking the vitals of a woman Rachel recognised immediately.

"She's alive, but only just. Rachel, run back, get help. We'll need an air ambulance, I think, unless they have rural 4x4s."

"I'm not happy leaving you here, Sarah. What if the person who did this is still around?"

"Rachel, I can't leave her. There's no phone signal and if she doesn't get help soon, she'll die. Please." Sarah's pleading eyes looked up from her patient momentarily. Rachel wasn't happy, but she knew her friend was right, and she also knew how fast she could run.

She turned and ran as fast as her legs could carry her, arriving ten minutes later back at the shuttle spot where she explained to the shocked tour guide what had happened.

Robert appeared from nowhere.

"It's your friend," Rachel told him. "She's badly injured. Sarah's trying to save her."

Two medics appeared, and Rachel and Robert followed them into their 4x4. Rachel guided them to where she had left Sarah.

"What are the injuries?" the paramedic who wasn't driving asked Rachel.

"I only saw her for a moment. My friend's a nurse so she stayed behind. It looked as though she'd been hit with a rock or something." Rachel grimaced and looked at Robert. "The side of her head was bleeding badly."

Robert put his head in his hands and she instinctively touched his shoulder. "Her husband needs to be told."

Robert stiffened.

Rachel continued to direct the driver until they arrived at the place where Sarah had been left behind. Relieved to see that Sarah was safe, Rachel observed the woman lying on the ground. Sarah had managed to stem the bleeding from her forehead and place her in the recovery position, but other than that, there was no change.

One paramedic opened his equipment bag while the other one grabbed items from him and checked the woman's vitals again.

"Her pulse is fifty-four, thready," said Sarah. "She's breathing on her own; pupils dilated with minimal reaction to light; she's not regained consciousness since we got here. Not sure if you use the Glasgow Coma Scale, but it's been 4, and she groaned once."

"Thanks, you're a nurse from the cruise ship, I believe?"

"Yes, I am."

"You may have saved her life. She's critical, though," the older paramedic said. He put an oxygen mask over the woman's face and turned on a portable oxygen cylinder.

The other man got on his medium-wave radio. "Air ambulance to Lake St Clair." He shouted out exact co-ordinates. "We'll also need the police – this woman's been a victim of a brutal attack."

Robert stood helplessly looking down at the woman, brushing back his hair and then prowling around, but giving the men room to work.

"Is she going to live?" His shaky voice finally uttered its first words since Rachel had bumped into him at the lakeside café.

"Not sure, mate, sorry, it's too early to tell. Do you know the woman?"

"Yes, she's, erm, a friend. Her husband is also a friend."

"We'll need some details, mate." One of the men questioned Robert and took down as much information as he could give; quite a lot, as it happened. Her name was Sunita Chowdry, aged thirty, married to Jack Chowdry, aged forty-two. No allergies as far as Robert knew and no serious illnesses.

"Has she been, erm, sexually assaulted?"

"Doesn't look like it, all clothing's intact – maybe it was a robbery. Her bag's not here. Was she carrying one?"

"I don't remember," said Robert.

Rachel knew he was lying about this as she'd seen him slip a note into Sunita's handbag before they boarded the shuttle bus. He glanced at her, frowning, and shot a warning look. Whatever was going on might have something to do with the case he was working on so Rachel held her tongue for now. A bulge in Sunita's pocket revealed her mobile phone was still on her person.

Helicopter blades disturbed the quiet countryside, and moments later Sunita was strapped into a stretcher and transferred to the air ambulance.

"Tell her husband she'll be at the North West Regional Hospital."

One of the paramedics boarded the air ambulance while the other headed back to the 4x4.

"Do you guys want a lift back?"

"I'll walk back, thanks, I need some air," said Robert.

"Okay, don't disturb the scene, though. The police will be here soon. They'll want to question you and search the area for clues."

Exactly what was Robert going to do? Rachel was going to stay behind and help him, but Sarah answered, "We'll have a lift, please. Come on, Rachel, I'll need to call this one back to the ship. You can speak to the police at lakeside or we'll stop on the way if we see them."

Rachel looked at Robert, but his back was turned. She followed Sarah into the waiting vehicle.

"Sarah," Robert called.

"Yes?"

"Thanks."

Sarah nodded acknowledgement and climbed up.

They were back at the lakeside within minutes, but by the time they'd given statements to the police, who also questioned the paramedic, it was too late to grab a drink as the shuttle was heading on to the visitor centre.

"I'll call Graham from there," Sarah said. "I'm not saying anything to Heel."

Sunita Chowdry's husband appeared from nowhere and others from his party rushed over to let him know the bad news. The police spent a few minutes speaking with him and a local offered to take him to town so that he could arrange to travel to the hospital. Rachel watched all of this very closely – he didn't look overly distressed.

"Are you thinking what I'm thinking?" Sarah was following Rachel's gaze.

"That he knew about the affair and attacked his wife thinking, you mean?"

"That's the one."

"It's a likely scenario along with three others."

"Which are?"

"The couple they had been watching are on to them and found Sunita out in the wilderness; she was attacked by a complete stranger; or—"

"Or she had arranged to meet Robert out there and he attacked her."

Rachel didn't answer, but it was a theory that had been running round in her head. If it was the case, she had left him out there to destroy evidence rather than find it. It didn't bear thinking about.

Once everyone was finally on board the shuttle bus, they were transferred back to the coach to continue with their tour. The police reassured the tour guide that they would ensure Robert made it back to the ship.

Rachel and Sarah tried hard to enjoy the rest of the day and take an interest in the visits, but they couldn't forget about the seriously injured woman they had come across. Sarah called the *Coral* and explained to Dr Bentley what had happened while Rachel tossed theories around. She watched the remaining three from Robert's group as they whispered and muttered to each other, clearly not knowing what to do without their leader and two of their colleagues. The couple they had been watching appeared oblivious, and if she hadn't known better, they would have looked like any other couple enjoying a wonderful holiday.

This cruise had just got even more complicated.

Chapter 19

The *Coral Queen* left port on time without Sunita and Jack Chowdry. Sarah just about had time to get changed before meeting the medical team, minus Alex who was dining with Greta in the officers' dining room. The team were empathetic about her day off turning into a busman's holiday once she had explained the morning's events, but Bernard couldn't resist teasing her.

"It's the Rachel Prince effect. What can you expect? Now we have her ex on board who seems to attract as much trouble as she does."

"So let me get this straight," interjected Graham. "Her ex-fiancé is a policeman from England who happens to be on the same ship as Rachel?"

"Sounds fishy to me," said Gwen.

"I thought so too, and so did Rachel, but now she reckons he's on some sort of covert mission following a couple who happen to be on this cruise. She also thinks he is having an affair with Sunita Chowdry." Sarah frowned, unsure whether Rachel would be happy about her sharing all this, but it would come out in one way or another anyway. Nobody really believed it was an attack by a stranger.

"Still, I think Rachel should be careful, because if her ex is involved in this attack, he'll know she'll work that out." Graham voiced what Sarah had been thinking. "If only Waverley were on board rather than this idiotic excuse for a chief of security." Graham slammed his napkin down on the table.

"Why isn't Captain Jenson doing anything about Heel's behaviour?" asked Brigitte. "He should be in the brig by now. I've heard there have been numerous complaints from staff."

Graham looked uncomfortable: he didn't like talking about a fellow senior officer, but Sarah guessed that he was wondering the same thing.

"I don't know. I've got to take Sarah's report about today's events over to Captain Jenson after dinner, so I'll ask him outright. It doesn't make any sense to me either. Gwen, ask Alex to do evening surgery and I'll catch you all later."

Graham rose from the table just as the pompous subject of their conversation entered. The rest of the team immediately rose and went to leave too, none of them wanting an encounter with the chief of security, least of all Sarah. Gwen had told her she wasn't to be alone with the man and Sarah had no intentions of going against her wishes. She hadn't seen Jason since the night before and hoped he really had got over what had been bothering him. Sarah was absolutely certain she had never encountered Chief Heel before in her life.

"Just a moment, you." Heel barred her way.

"What can I do for you, Officer Heel?" Sarah tried to control herself, but it was no use. Her hands were clearly trembling.

"I need to talk to you about what happened today, and other matters," he snarled.

Gwen intervened. "Nurse Bradshaw is late for surgery, so if you want to speak to her, come to my office at seven-thirty prompt." She then took Sarah's arm and led her around the shocked figure of Chief Heel.

"Remind me not to get on your wrong side," laughed Sarah.

"A point you'll do well to remember," replied Gwen in good humour. "That man is terrifying too many people, I do hope Graham has some success with the captain."

Evening surgery passed by quickly, although Sarah was finding it difficult to concentrate, dreading the meeting with the CSO – if he turned up as Gwen had instructed.

She needn't have worried, though. When she arrived at Gwen's office, there was no sign of the chief, but her face lit up when she found Jason waiting outside for her. Against their usual discretion, they flew into each other's arms and she buried her head in his chest.

"Oh Jason, am I glad to see you." The tears that had been welling up since yesterday now flowed freely down his shirt.

"I heard you had a bad day." He stroked her wavy hair soothingly. The smell of him and the feeling of safety at being in his arms caused her to cry hysterically, and Gwen came storming out of her office.

"Oh, it's you, Jason, sorry. I thought it was that horrible man, Heel. Why don't you two use my office for a while? I've got to go and see Raggie about some supplies." As medical steward, Raggie was a valued member of the team who always seemed to know what they needed and when, from coffee to food, to space.

Jason led Sarah through into Gwen's office and sat her down on the settee, pouring her a coffee from the jug that was always available at the end of a surgery. He then sat next to her and pulled her close.

"I'm sorry, I was a fool to think you would hide anything from me. It's Heel, he's poison, said horrible things about Graham and you – things I couldn't process – and my insecurity kicked in."

"Jason, I love you. I don't want to be with anyone else but you and I really don't know why your chief thinks he knows me. He doesn't. There's something more to it, I'm sure. I think he's unbalanced."

Jason breathed slowly and she could feel every breath as he held her. She didn't want this moment to end.

"I love you too, Sarah Bradshaw. I've been a bit slow off the mark and I should have told you a lot sooner."

As Sarah lifted her head from his chest and gazed into his dark blue eyes, noticing the hint of a tear, she felt breathless, but happier than she had ever felt in her life.

"I see you two have made up." Bernard was grinning from ear to ear as he walked in, followed closely behind by Brigitte. He punched Jason on the arm. "Come to your senses at last, man."

Brigitte snorted. "Men! They are always so slow to realise when they have a good woman. You don't deserve us."

They all laughed as Brigitte's usual take on the topic of men caused the male faces to redden, and even Bernard didn't fire back his trademark quip. He just smiled happily.

"Coffee anyone?" he asked.

"Did someone say coffee?" Alex joined them and, looking around at the happy faces, added, "Have I missed something?" while throwing himself down on one of Gwen's chairs. "Gwen will be here in a minute. She's asked us to stick around – you too, Jason. Graham's on his way back from seeing the captain."

Thank goodness for that, thought Sarah. Hopefully it's good news.

Chapter 20

Rachel ordered a burger meal from the room service menu, a pot of coffee and tiramisu to follow. Having opened the folder she'd taken from Mrs F's suite and spread out the papers across the coffee table in her room, she looked for anything of significance.

There was a long list of the tour party passengers with five columns beside each name where Florence Flanders had made meticulous notes. A column headed 'Medical' included notes on allergies, illnesses and medication, followed by one headed 'Food' where she had listed dietary requirements, including likes and dislikes. The third column was headed 'Activities' and detailed the tours and classes each bucket lister was booked on to. Rachel noticed her self-defence class on the list and tried not to get sidetracked.

In the fourth column were the bucket listers' preferred names. Patty's full name was Patricia, but that came as no surprise, and Glenis went by her middle name, her first name being Trudy. Manandeep Janda's preferred name was not listed as Deep, and while Rachel wondered why that might be, she didn't feel it was significant.

The final column was the one that had her puzzled most of all because it didn't have a heading. Florence had added question marks beside some of the names and crosses beside others.

Dinner arrived while ideas danced around in her head about the meaning of this last column. Some question marks were in red and some were in light blue – what did that mean? Potential suitors? No, that couldn't be it as there were both men and women on the list. Six question marks were circled – that would be the place to start.

Rachel pushed the papers away and laid her tray of food on the table. She picked up the huge burger that was sandwiched in a roll with cheese, salad and coleslaw and bit into it, almost choking on the hot barbecue relish that made her eyes water, but quickly adjusted to the surprising amount of heat. A burger was not her usual choice of food as she much preferred healthy options and rarely ate this much fat in one sitting, but neither she nor Sarah had been able to face food when they had eventually arrived at their lunch stop on the outing, still shocked by the Sunita Chowdry episode.

Rachel sat back in the chair and replayed the day's events in her head. Robert had looked shocked by the attack, but was that because he did actually have feelings for Sunita Chowdry? Or had he known where she was and been surprised at her being found, and more surprised she was alive, albeit only just?

Having dealt with a few incidents such as this in her day job as a police officer, Rachel knew that the woman's chances were slim, and even if she did regain consciousness, she might never be the same person again. Personality changes were common with head injuries, but the most scary was the complete loss of memory in relation to loved ones. Rachel had attended an RTA where the injured man couldn't remember he was married and had flirted inappropriately with the nurses – the doctors tried to explain to his wife that the brain damage had affected the prefrontal cortex that controls inhibition, but the man had become totally uninhibited, exposing himself, swearing and making lewd comments to all and sundry. His wife couldn't believe that her quiet husband, who'd never sworn and had always been decent, had become someone she would normally have nothing to do with. Sadly the marriage ended in divorce and the man never recovered, ending up in a long-term care facility. At least Rachel had the satisfaction of arresting the woman responsible for the hit and run: a woman who had been drinking on the eve of the accident and ploughed into the young man, leaving him to be found by a passing motorist.

Thinking back to this morning, Rachel remembered she and Sarah had passed a number of people on their walk, but none after they'd left the boardwalk. Whoever the culprit was had left the scene before they arrived. She shuddered at the thought of being found dead behind a boulder in a strange country – who had done this to Sunita?

Robert was a pain in the butt, and had treated Rachel abominably by taking up with another woman, but he was now revealing a philanderer's trait she'd had no idea he possessed before meeting up with him again on this cruise. He'd clearly moved on from controlling to putting himself about, but was he capable of attempted murder? That was for the police to find out; she was certain Chief Heel would be incapable of solving a crime of this magnitude. From what she'd seen of him, his investigative skills were little to none.

No doubt the Australian police would be around when the ship docked in Melbourne the next morning. They would need to work quickly as this was the final Australia stop before the ship headed to New Zealand for the rest of the cruise.

After finishing her meal and downing a full pot of coffee, Rachel put the tray outside her door on the floor for the stewards to take away and returned to the papers scattered around the table.

"Now back to the question marks."

Forty-five minutes later, when she was no wiser, her mobile phone rang. She didn't recognise the number, but answered anyway.

"Hello?"

"Rachel, it's me."

"How did you get this number?" Stupid question, she had never changed her number, but she had barred Robert from calling. He'd obviously changed his.

"Do I really need to answer that?"

The self-satisfied smugness infuriated her.

"No. Anyway, what is it? I'm busy."

"You're not the placid, shy girl I once knew, Rachel. I like that, you've matured."

Inexplicable anger took over. "Unlike you, still the same wannabe control freak you always were, not to mention the wandering eye."

"I can't help it if women find me irresistible," he snapped back.

Now I've riled him, not to mention myself, this will get us nowhere. Rachel felt her usual calm return, satisfied enough that she had finally got to tell him what she thought of him, even if it was not as thoroughly as she would have liked.

"Sure, Robert, if you say so." She couldn't prevent the sarcasm sneaking out of her mouth. He was bringing out the worst in her, even though the anger had quieted.

"Look, I need to see you."

"And that's not going to happen."

"What room are you in?"

"What part of 'No' didn't you hear?"

"I could find out, you know, I have contacts on the ship."

"Who might they be?"

"Just kidding."

She'd managed to goad him into slipping something out he hadn't intended her to know. She would need to find out who his contacts were.

"Why do you need to see me?"

"It's about Sunita, I need to explain."

"You don't need to explain to me, Robert. I'm not the one you married, remember?"

"Come on, Rachel, give me a break. I'm upset, and you care about me deep down. You know you do."

Did he really think this boyish charm was going to work on her? Her hand trembled as she spoke through gritted teeth.

"That train left the station a long time ago, literally. I don't mean you harm, Robert, but I don't want anything to do with you. Take your problems elsewhere."

"Who do you think you're talking to? You're just a bitter woman. You'll regret this conversation."

"Not half as much as I regret not seeing through you years ago." If it was possible to slam down a mobile phone, she would have done it. Instead, she pressed the call-end button and threw the phone across the room.

No longer in the mood to look through the papers and wondering if she had gone too far with Robert, she washed the day's stresses away in the shower and changed into a cocktail dress ready to meet Sarah. Sitting back in the chair, feeling calmer, she pondered the conversation with Robert and chastised herself for being taken in by him in the first place. Now she was a little older and wiser, she was sure she wouldn't have fallen for him if she'd met him today, but then he'd only ever showed her the charming side of his nature, so how could she have known?

Thoughts of Carlos returned. With Carlos, what you saw was what you got. His eyes oozed kindness; he helped people without expecting anything in return; he even took on some clients without pay. Robert would never have done that. What's more, she felt a deeper bond with Carlos than she'd ever done with Robert. Infatuation, that's what it had been.

A knock at the stateroom door shocked her from her thoughts. How the heck had Robert found out where she was staying so quickly? With a dead weight filling her stomach and struggling to control her breathing, she walked cautiously across the room.

Clenching her fists ready to do battle, Rachel looked through the spy hole in the door and her mouth dropped open.

Chapter 21

On entering senior nurse Gwen Sumner's office, Rachel laughed as she saw the same reaction she had had on seeing the visitor who was now accompanying her. It was like looking at goldfish in a bowl as every mouth opened in disbelief.

Dr Bentley was the first to speak, standing up and rushing towards them.

"Jack, my dear fellow, am I pleased to see you."

"Sorry to startle you all like this, I understand you've been having some problems with the new man."

"Understatement of the year," said Gwen. "Chief Waverley, can I get you a coffee?"

"Something a bit stronger, if you don't mind – brandy?" He sat down in one of the chairs.

Jason stood. "Good to see you, sir."

"And you, Goodridge."

Rachel remained standing, still confused as Waverley hadn't explained his presence since arriving unexpectedly at her door.

Waverley coughed in his usual way before beginning an explanation. "I thought I'd collect Miss Prince on the way, knowing she would be involved."

"Come on, Jack, the tension's killing us. What's going on? Where's Brenda?" asked Dr Bentley.

After taking a small drink of brandy, clearly enjoying himself, Waverley launched into his explanation.

"About six weeks ago, the captain called me into his accommodation off the Bridge and told me about a security chief on a sister ship who was causing all sorts of problems. No-one knew whether it was sour grapes as he'd been employed at the expense of the promotion of their deputy, but due to his rather odd behaviour, and knowing I was due to take some leave to go on honeymoon, Captain Jenson asked if I would do some background checks while I was away and recommend the chief joined this ship to cover my leave."

"Of course we are speaking about Brian Heel?" Gwen clarified.

"Yes, but the only people who knew about this plan were the captain, myself and Charlotte Franks, my deputy."

"I wondered why she hadn't been left in charge," said Dr Bentley.

"Well, in many ways, she has been. She's been observing and diarising Heel's behaviour all the time he's been on board. She's also been trying to investigate the murder of the passenger found in the library – something we hadn't anticipated," he coughed, "although in light of Miss Prince being on board, we should have."

Rachel gave Sarah a 'don't you dare laugh' look, which she – and everyone else – totally ignored, so Rachel rolled her eyes until the guffaws around the room had subsided.

Once the laughter quieted, Waverley continued. "As our man had been in the Norwegian navy rather than the British, I had to call in some favours from an old friend – I won't bore you with the details of why he owed me. Suffice it to say we were on a joint operation some years ago and I saved his bacon." Waverley took another sip of brandy.

"We thought you were in the Caribbean," said Bernard.

"I'll have to save that for another time, sadly."

"And?" Sarah asked impatiently.

"Brian Heel's case is a sad one, I'm afraid. He's gay – not something they concern themselves with in the Norwegian forces, unlike ours. Unfortunately, his partner, also a sailor, had an accident while out on the rifle range. He was shot by a friendly bullet – I've never understood that term, no bullet is friendly, but that's the term used so we'll live with it for now. They were out in the wilds somewhere in the forests of Norway, and Heel saw his friend fall.

"The only medic around there was a nurse. The poor woman did her best, but she couldn't bring the man round; he had died instantly. Heel could never accept it;

177

apparently, he tried to get the nurse thrown out of the navy for negligence. When he didn't succeed with that, he smeared her name all over the camp, making up false stories about her. In the end, she had a breakdown and left the navy anyway.

"Still not satisfied, he started on other nurses. In fact, my old pal found out he must have been having flashbacks, imagining every nurse he met was the nurse that he maintained had killed his partner because she couldn't save him. He was given a dishonourable discharge in the end, and then somehow managed to lie his way into employment with a smaller cruise line at first, and now Queen Cruises."

"How did he get through the background checks?" asked Jason, pulling Sarah towards him, clearly realising how much she must have suffered as Heel had dug his knives into her.

"An old officer, who felt sorry for him, gave him the references he needed. He behaved for a while, even on our sister ship, but started to become agitated recently, snarling at crew and passengers."

"Especially nurses?" Rachel asked.

"No, in fact, he steered clear of the medical centre. It seems our dead body and Sarah's presence with the team unable to save the poor woman triggered a dangerous chain reaction. He's been much worse since being on board the *Coral Queen* by all accounts. Charlotte has been having Sarah watched in case he posed any physical danger. I'm sorry, Sarah, we had no idea how bad this would get. He's clearly suffering from some sort of post-traumatic stress, so he's now under house arrest. Graham, he won't take kindly to you assessing him so we've called in a mental health expert who'll see him when we get to Melbourne. If he won't receive help, the plan is to repatriate him to Norway where he can be assessed by medics there."

The team and Rachel were quiet as they digested the information. In retrospect, the signs were obvious, but a real and present mental health problem had slipped through their grasp.

"Well, let's hope the poor man gets the help he requires." Dr Bentley spoke for them all.

"Are you staying?" Gwen asked Waverley.

"I wasn't going to, but as we have one murder and one attempted murder on our hands, I feel I must. Brenda's meeting the ship tomorrow and will join me. I married a very understanding wife. Anyway it's high time she got back to baking for passengers, I've put on far too much weight." He rubbed his expanding abdomen.

"Married life suits you," said Sarah. Other than that, she had been very quiet.

"One down, two to go," said Rachel happily.

"What do you mean?" asked Waverley.

"Investigations." She flopped herself down onto the settee in Gwen's office and put her arm around Sarah protectively.

Waverley groaned before giving Rachel a hard stare. "Miss Prince, may I remind you that you are a guest lecturer on board this ship, NOT a member of the security team. You are not to have anything else to do with either of the ongoing investigations, and if I find you meddling I will have you placed under house arrest. Do I make myself clear?"

Waverley's tone was sharper than usual and the redness extending from his neck to his face convinced Rachel he was serious. Perhaps having his honeymoon interrupted had made him less tolerant, or perhaps it was Brian Heel's behaviour rubbing off on him.

"Quite clear, Chief." She resisted the urge to salute and exchanged a quick glance with Jason, who of course knew about the loot in her stateroom.

"In that case, I bid you all good evening. Goodridge, I need to see you."

After the two men had left, Gwen broke the astonished silence, smiling sympathetically. "Well that's you put in your place, *Miss* Prince."

"I think he's serious this time, Rachel," said Dr Bentley. "You really should stay out of this one."

Rachel nodded slowly, thoughts elsewhere.

"Come along, *Miss* Prince, let's get a drink." Sarah pulled Rachel up from the chair.

"No more Miss Prince business or you're buying." Rachel nudged Sarah, who looked back into the room.

"Is anyone else joining us?"

Bernard was out of his seat like a shot, but Dr Bentley declined.

"Gwen and I have some papers to go over and I've got to be up early tomorrow. My sons and their families are joining and I promised them a tour of the ship." Dr Bentley's face lit up as if he'd only just remembered. "I must say I'm jolly pleased we won't be having to tiptoe around Heel while they are on board. Waverley has his faults, but he's a decent chap so we'll be back to normal now."

Rachel wasn't quite convinced that would be the case, but didn't want to burst Dr Bentley's bubble.

Alex explained he was meeting Greta for drinks, bringing an eyebrow raise from Dr Bentley who was slow off the mark when it came to his team's love interests. Brigitte was quiet, which was not like her, so Rachel looked at her.

"Are you coming, Brigitte."

"I never turn down a drink, although it will be lemonade for me. I'm on call." The smile didn't reach her eyes and the usual joviality of the French nurse was missing. Rachel wondered if the others had noticed and whether Sarah knew what was wrong with her. She would ask later.

The quartet opted to go for a drink in the main atrium for a change and listen to a folk trio at the same time. They found a table next to one of the internal windows, close enough to hear the band singing but far enough away to have a quiet conversation without being overheard. The nurses were still in their whites and didn't like to draw attention to themselves – another reason for finding a table on the periphery.

Rachel looked out on the dark evening sky; the sun had long disappeared. She had watched from her room earlier as the large orange orb sank below the edge of the horizon. While the nurses were discussing their day and sharing funny stories, she was only half listening.

Sarah was describing the good things they had seen in Burnie while Bernard told jokes about his encounter with an elderly woman who had fallen off a barstool after drinking too much brandy. She had told Bernard that the last time she had drunk so much was at her husband's funeral. Bernard said he'd asked her if it was grief or a final farewell, and she had replied that it was a celebratory toast at getting rid of the miserable old devil.

Rachel heard this last part of the conversation and joined in the laughter.

"Bernard, I'm sure you make these stories up," laughed Sarah.

Bernard straightened up and pouted. "I do not. People confide in me. Anyway, she brightened up my day. We had just heard the news about that poor young woman you found."

"I don't want to do this job anymore." Brigitte broke through the humour.

Sarah gawped at her, truly astonished. "Why ever not? You love this work."

"Not to mention me," said Bernard, clearly trying to chivvy his friend and colleague out of her mood, but all it did was draw a scowl.

"I'm homesick, I want to be back in my beautiful country and have a normal relationship with a romantic Frenchman."

Rachel reflected on the pain she had felt after leaving home for the first time, but Brigitte had been working for Queen Cruises for a few years now. She surmised it was more about the relationship desire than the homesickness. Brigitte, Sarah had told her, had always been aloof to members of the opposite sex on board the *Coral Queen*, fearing the ship gossip rounds that spread like wildfire when a new relationship struck up.

Sarah cut to the chase. "This is about Novak, isn't it?"

Brigitte lifted her head and her eyes darted wildly. "How did you know?"

"Know what?" asked Bernard, clearly confused by the sudden knowing looks passing between his two female friends. Rachel smiled as she watched the different reactions.

"It doesn't take a rocket scientist," Sarah continued, ignoring Bernard.

"Know what?" he persisted.

"Men!" Brigitte glared at Bernard. "You know nothing, all you care about is football."

Brigitte's scathing reply drew laughter from the rest of them.

"What are you all laughing about? It's not funny."

Rachel put her arm around her friend. "The Brigitte we know and love is back."

"If you must know, he's asked me out seven-and-a-half times."

Bernard spluttered his drink across the table. "Seven-and-a-*half* times?"

"The half was today. He'd just managed to say, 'Please go out' when Graham came along and he shuffled away – coward that he is."

"Ah, kettle and pot come to mind. Come on, Brigitte, face it: you're scared," Sarah said gently.

Realisation crossed Bernard's face. "She's scared of it not working out, is that it? If you want my opinion, it's time you took some risks. If it's the Novak I'm thinking of from the casino, he's a good man and I've not known him ask anyone out before. Maybe you're both scared."

"No-one asked for your opinion, Bernard relationship guidance counsellor – *not*." Brigitte glared at him, but broke into a grin when he sat back in his chair, triumphantly unperturbed.

"Bernard's right," said Sarah. "I can tell you like him and he is drooling over you – what have you got to lose?"

"My reputation." Brigitte looked down into her lap.

Bernard was prevented from making his next quip when Sarah kicked him under the table.

"Ow! What was that for?"

Sarah's raised eyebrows had the desired effect and Bernard held his tongue.

"What do you think, Rachel? You don't work on the ship. Should I get involved?"

Rachel paused thoughtfully before answering. "I get what you're afraid of, but in many ways, it's no different to dating anyone from work really. I wouldn't advise you either way, but if you do like this man and you keep refusing him, he might stop asking, and then how would you feel?"

"What if it fails?"

Sarah took her friend's hand. "If it fails, you move on, and your friends will be around to support you. Won't we, Bernard?"

"Of course we will, we'll always have each other's backs. Give it a try. You will never know if you don't try. And, although you think we men have no feelings, I can tell you from experience, it takes great courage to ask a woman out, knowing she has the power to say yes or no. If she says yes, we float on air, and if she says no, it's one more dent to our fragile confidence. If he's asked you out seven-and-a-half times, he's an idiot or he recognises your struggle and your 'no's have not been clear enough. Don't keep him hanging on, it's not fair – either say no and mean it or say yes."

"Maybe he just doesn't listen," Brigitte retaliated.

"I've seen you with him, Brigitte, there's chemistry," said Sarah. "Bernard's right, you're not being fair on him."

"Since when does Bernard get the monopoly on being right? And he certainly doesn't know anything about fragile confidence," said Brigitte, laughing. "I'll think about it and make a final decision before I see him again."

"Well that final decision had better be quick."

Rachel followed Bernard's eye line and observed a small, lean man with a mop of curly black hair heading through the atrium. Although he hadn't seen them, Brigitte leapt from her seat and followed after him, and they headed towards the spiral stairs leading up to the casino, deep in conversation. Rachel assumed the man was Novak, who was taking the heavy on-call bag from Brigitte and carrying it upstairs for her.

"Only two more to go," said Bernard, unable to conceal his excitement.

Sarah was still smiling and missed what he said, but Rachel knew what he meant. Remembering their conversation on boarding day, she recognised he was referring to the fact that now only Dr Bentley and Gwen on the medical team remained single.

Chapter 22

After Bernard had left them, Rachel and Sarah made their way into the Jazz Bar. Almost as soon as they sat down in a booth, an unwelcome visitor sat opposite.

"Where have you been? I've been waiting for hours," Robert asked. Rachel looked aghast at the effrontery of the man. Sarah looked at her, questioning whether she had agreed a meeting without telling her.

"You've got a nerve! I told you I had no intention of meeting with you."

"And I told you I'd find you."

Rachel sighed heavily and decided this conversation was going to be a repeat of their earlier battle unless she took the heat out of it. Robert would never back down. Men and their testosterone levels – no wonder there was so much violence in the world.

"What do you want, Robert?"

He leaned forward, relaxing a little now that he felt he had won. He looked at Sarah, as if weighing up whether to ask her to leave, but Rachel nipped that in the bud.

"Anything you have to say will be said in front of Sarah. That's the deal for me hearing you out – take it or leave it."

He opened his mouth as if to counter, but obviously decided not to push.

"I think I'm in trouble."

"Why?" asked Rachel.

Sarah had stiffened from the moment Robert arrived, but now she was listening, both women waiting for Robert to continue.

Robert looked down at his hands, clearly weighing up how much to say.

"I'm working on a case, and it seems to have gone pear shaped."

"You or a team of you are working on a case?" Rachel pressed.

"I have a team. All the guys and gals you've seen with me are undercover police officers, working with me on it. It involves major international money laundering and stolen antiquity smuggling. We've been working with the border force, trying to find out how far it goes and who's at the top. We were given a tip off a few weeks ago that a couple taking this cruise would be meeting up with the head of operations, but we had no idea whether this head would be a fellow passenger or someone at one of the ports. We don't think it's a crew member."

"So you've been watching the couple to see who they speak to," Rachel interjected. "But you took your eye off the ball today, didn't you?"

Robert shifted uncomfortably in his seat. "We have to be careful not to be seen watching them so we take turns, and it wasn't my turn." His jaw stuck out, his expression moving from embarrassed to defensive.

"You decided to meet up with Sunita while her husband was on watch." It was a statement rather than a question and Rachel found it difficult to hide her disgust.

"Alright, Miss Prim and Proper, yes, I did, but when I got to the meeting place, she was lying there."

Sarah gasped. "You left her out there to die?"

"I didn't realise she was alive – I panicked. I would never have left her if I thought that I could save her, you have to believe that."

"Why should we believe you? And even if you thought she was dead, you should have done the decent thing and called for help. Her husband had a right to know." Sarah's voice had gone up by a number of decibels. Rachel was worried Robert would clam up or get aggressive, but he covered his face with his hands.

"Look, you're right, that's what I should have done, and now I know she was alive all along, I wish I could turn the clock back. What you don't know is that I found some of my personal stuff lying around. She even had a broken chain in her hand." He paused, his voice breaking. "It was mine – someone hit her over the head and tried to frame me for the murder. I suspect whoever did this thought she was dead too."

"If it wasn't you – and trust me, Robert, I'm not totally convinced it wasn't – then who do you think it was?"

"It can only be Jack. Maybe he found out, although we were very careful."

Rachel remembered how indiscreet they had been at the coach drop off point, but said nothing.

"Or the couple we have been following?" Robert continued.

"Why would they try to kill Sunita?"

"I don't know, I've been racking my brains trying to think why. Perhaps she stumbled across them meeting with the ringleader and they had no choice."

"Except that would indicate an impromptu attack. They wouldn't have been able to try framing you – unless—"

"Unless what?" asked Sarah.

"Unless the hunter has become the hunted," said Rachel. Robert's face told her he didn't buy it, but she persevered. "Think about it, Robert. What if they found out, or even had a tip off themselves that they were being watched. If the ringleader is on the ship, he or she could have been watching you watching them, and believe me, you were not nearly as careful as you think you were with regards to Sunita. I worked that one out fairly early. It was confirmed by your childish behaviour and secret notes when the coach stopped this morning."

Robert's face went ashen. "I don't believe you."

"She's telling the truth," confirmed Sarah. "I hadn't noticed, but Rachel pointed the two of you out and it didn't take a genius to work out what you were up to."

"I still don't believe they're on to us, it has to be Jack."

"How well do you know him? Is he capable of attempting to kill his wife?" asked Rachel.

"I don't think so, but there's no other explanation."

"I don't think he suspected." Rachel took a drink from the Martini and lemonade that had arrived while they were talking.

"So now you're an expert in detective work, are you? Look, Rachel, I've been doing this job for a few years now, and I was a sergeant when you were still a probationer, remember that."

Sarah opened her mouth, about to launch into a tirade, but Rachel stopped her. She still wasn't absolutely certain Robert was telling the truth and didn't want to warn him off. If he thought she was good at solving murders, he might run away.

"Humour me. What if the gang is on to you? It would make perfect sense to frame you, the boss – remove the head and all that – and perhaps they don't have any qualms about killing someone in the process."

"If it was the suspects, I still think it was opportunistic. Sunita could have found out something by accident."

"So they attacked her and randomly found items belonging to you and scattered them about." Sarah's disdain for Robert had turned into ridicule. "Come on, Detective, explain that," she challenged.

Robert turned thoughtful. "I need to think about this – if you're right, I'd better not be seen with you in case someone thinks you're part of the investigation." He got up abruptly before turning back. "But my money's on Jack."

"Arrogant fool," muttered Sarah as Robert walked away.

Rachel didn't reply; she was deep in thought. Things had become even more complicated and she was facing a dilemma. Waverley had already warned her off, but she now had two tantalising cases tormenting her.

She looked up and saw Glenis and company seated at a table in the centre of the bar. Glenis and Prudence waved, so Rachel smiled at them and raised her glass in salutation. Emma scowled and Patty looked as confused as ever.

Sarah turned her head to follow Rachel's gaze.

"Ah, the bucket list tour. Rachel, I know you find puzzles intriguing, but I do hope you're going to heed Waverley's advice."

"Since when have I refused to follow advice?" Rachel smirked and Sarah frowned.

"This other case sounds dangerous, please stay out of it. Do you believe scumbag?"

Rachel laughed at the reference to Robert, but then turned serious.

"I think so. Robert might be a philanderer, but I don't see him as a murderer, and anyway, he looked happy with Sunita, behaving like a couple of teenagers. He'd have no reason to attack her. He's probably right. It would be much more likely to be someone she knew than this gang they're tracking. Antiquity theft and murder are poles apart."

"Except large sums of money would be involved, and you know as well as I do how money often plays a part in murder."

"As does jealousy," said Rachel.

"Do you think you should tell Waverley?"

"Why me? Why don't you tell him? Anyway I can't because if it is an undercover operation, cruise ship security will be either in the know or deliberately left out of the loop, and there will be compelling reasons for both."

"That sounds like a cop out to me." Sarah smiled. "As for me, I'm delighted to have the gruff Waverley back. He's infinitely preferable to Brian Heel."

"I'll drink to that." Rachel raised her glass and both women took a large gulp from their drinks. "One more thing, I'm pleased you and Jason have made up."

"Mmm."

"What does that mean?"

"He doubted me, Rachel. He listened to Heel and didn't even tell me what had been said; he just blanked me and pushed me away. It doesn't do a lot for a girl's confidence. I thought we were making headway, now I'm not so sure."

Rachel understood where Sarah was coming from and in many ways she was right, but she also recognised that Jason had trust issues stemming back years. Issues that she herself had had after Robert's betrayal. She sometimes wondered if she would ever trust Carlos as she had once trusted Robert.

"Perhaps he needs a little more time," she answered Sarah wistfully.

Sarah squeezed her hand as Glenis came over to join them, accompanied by Prudence, Charles, Deep and Patty.

"Come on, spill the beans. Who was that handsome hunk you were talking to?" asked Prudence.

Rachel kicked Sarah under the table before she could say anything. "Someone we met a couple of days ago and then again on the tour today. I think he's with a mixed group of friends."

Sarah took up the baton. "He was asking about the woman who had the accident today."

"Yes, terrible thing to happen, she fell on the rocks according to the tour guide and had to be taken to hospital," Charles said. "It's dangerous when you move off the recommended paths."

Rachel perked up. Was that a warning in his tone or had she imagined it?

"These things happen in threes, I wonder who's next," said Patty, staring into space.

"Don't be silly, Patty," said Glenis. "People have accidents, it's just one of those things."

"Well I'm beginning to wonder how many of us will make it off this ship alive. When I joined a bucket list tour, I wasn't meaning it literally," Prudence remarked sombrely.

"Don't be so overdramatic," said Charles. "Anyway, nothing will happen to you ladies – I'm your protector, remember." He winked at Prudence, who blushed.

"What are you two doing tomorrow?" asked Glenis.

"I'm working, I'm afraid," answered Sarah.

Deep stared at Rachel, awaiting a response.

"I haven't decided."

"Please join us. We are going on a private tour of the Yarra Valley," begged Glenis.

Rachel looked unsure.

"Yes, do, Rachel. It would be lovely to have you along, wouldn't it, gang?" said Charles.

Rachel choked on her drink at the thought of this group of kindly pensioners being in a gang. "In that case, yes. I would be honoured."

"Perhaps you can teach us some self-defence on the way."

Deep raised his eyebrows quizzically.

"Rachel is the self-defence teacher – black belt in karate, you know, so be careful," Prudence teased.

"Oh, I most certainly will," retorted Deep.

Charles smiled affectionately at Prudence. "I have a few moves of my own, you know."

"I think I'm going to throw up," interrupted Emma, joining the group in time to hear the last part of the conversation. "Come on, Patty. Time to go."

The muddled woman dutifully got up and followed after the stick insect.

"Where did she come from?" asked Glenis.

"I think she'd been to the ladies," answered Prudence.

"Anyway, I apologise, but I can't keep up with your gang," said Rachel. "I'll see you in the morning."

Sarah got up too. "Goodnight, enjoy your day out tomorrow."

"Goodnight," the group answered in unison before returning to their conversations.

"That should keep you out of mischief," said Sarah.

"I wondered why you looked so pleased when they invited me."

"Why didn't you want to let on that you knew Robert?"

"I'm not sure, really. Partly because I didn't want to explain about an ex or I'd be quizzed to death, and partly because there has still been a murder within the bucket list tour group. Deep already knows who Robert is, having rescued me on the first day, but he will respect my privacy."

"I can't say I blame you, they would have wanted to know all the nitty gritty details, I'm sure. You don't suspect any of them of being involved in the murder of Mrs F, do you?"

"Based on previous experience, no-one can be ruled out of a murder investigation until all the facts are uncovered. I think the clues lie in Florence Flanders's notes somewhere but I have to give everything back to Jason tonight."

"Just remember this is a murder investigation that you are not going to pursue, Rachel Prince."

The women laughed and linked arms as they made their way towards the lifts before parting to go to their respective staterooms.

Chapter 23

The following morning, Rachel met with Deep in the buffet for breakfast before they headed off to join the rest of the gang in the main atrium. Deep looked frailer each time she saw him and the faraway look in his eyes refused to yield, even when Rachel tried to distract him. He remained polite but distant and was likely to stay that way until this business with Florence Flanders was over and he was allowed to return home.

It is a pity to be visiting some of the most beautiful parts of the world and not see what is right before his eyes, thought Rachel. At least he was still joining in even if he was not the man she had met just a few days ago. It made her more determined than ever to ignore Waverley's advice and get to the bottom of the murder of his friend.

"And then there's the business of Georgia. Who drugged her?"

"Pardon?" Deep looked confused.

"Sorry, I didn't realise I'd spoken out loud, I was lost in thought." Rachel looked around to check no-one else had heard.

"You meant Georgia Flanders, didn't you?"

"Yes, sorry. I can't help thinking that whoever drugged her had a part in her grandmother's murder."

"I see you're like me, Rachel. Neither of us can dismiss the events of a few days ago, and yet life seems to go on for everyone else as if nothing happened. Why is it that people don't care?"

"I'm sure people care, but they are on holiday and it wasn't the most pleasant of beginnings for them either. Remember, this is their bucket list cruise, something they always wanted to do before they die. We shouldn't deny them that pleasure, and it's not as if they knew Mrs Flanders. The initial shock has waned, that's all."

"You are wise beyond your years, Rachel Prince. I wish we had met under happier circumstances; I'm afraid I'm not much company now as all I want to do is go home."

"Will you tell your wife?"

"I don't think so, it would only cause friction and needless pain. My children would not be happy with me for chasing an old flame, no matter how much I try to convince myself my intentions were honourable."

Rachel wanted to hug him and encourage him to cry; the tears were constantly beneath the surface, but he was too proud or stubborn to let them out.

"I believe you would have behaved honourably, even if that wasn't your intention," she said gently.

"Can I ask you something, Rachel?"

"Yes, of course."

"Why do you care so much? Is it your Christian upbringing?"

"I'm sure that's part of it, my father always encouraged me and my brother to right a wrong if it was within our power to do so." She laughed. "I guess I've taken it to another level."

"Is that why you joined the police force?"

"I almost forgot you know I am a police officer."

"Even if I hadn't known, that chief of security, Chief Heel, was not very discreet, but don't worry, I haven't told anyone else. I gathered you wanted it kept secret."

"Why didn't he just get a loudspeaker and announce it to the world?" she snapped. "Thank you for understanding."

"I rarely tell anyone I was a doctor, for the same reasons probably. As soon as people realise, they insist on reciting their full medical history in horrifying detail." It was Deep's turn to laugh.

They arrived at the main atrium and Glenis immediately commandeered Rachel, taking her arm and pulling her towards Prudence, Victor and Charles. Rachel grimaced as she saw Emma and Patty not too far away, speaking to the South African group from the open mic night. She didn't mind Patty, but Emma was another story.

Before long they were boarding a private minibus for their tour. There were sixteen people from the bucket list group, plus Rachel. She followed Glenis and her small travelling party towards the back of the luxury vehicle where they found seats, and thankfully Deep sat next to her rather than Emma.

"I must pay something towards my being here."

"Don't you worry about that, dear. We hired the coach and I knew there was a space because Joe told me last night," said Glenis from the seat behind, where she was sitting next to Prudence. Charles and Victor sat across the aisle from Rachel, with Emma and Patty in front of the two men. "Joe's accompanying us on this one – here he is now."

This was the first time Rachel had come across Joe Flanders close up and she studied him. He was perhaps an inch taller than she was, and his face was round yet sharp. The nicest thing about him was his baby blue eyes. His clothing was smart casual: he wore a light beige suit with blue shirt and no tie. The trousers were chinos.

"Good morning, all, I trust you are well and enjoying your cruise. We have a very exciting day for you today, but it will be a long one."

"How long?" asked Patty. "I don't like long trips."

Emma glared at Joe and said sharply, "It won't be that long, and remember we're going on the steam train."

"Oh, I love steam trains, they remind me of my time in India—"

"Yes, well, enough of that for now." Emma turned and glared at Rachel, or was it Deep she had glared at? It was all too quick to be certain, but Rachel supposed either way it was because the woman wasn't happy with her presence.

"What is her problem?" she muttered as she turned to look out of the window.

Joe reeled in control of the conversation and answered a few logistical questions before returning to the front, where he sat just behind the driver.

Rachel watched passengers walking down the three sets of makeshift stairs erected at intervals along the ship on the dockside. Her interest was piqued when she spotted the couple that Robert's group were staking out, but she could see no sign of Robert or his colleagues. The couple boarded a sister minibus parked next to theirs, shared by other members of the bucket list tour party.

How odd!

As she watched them, she noticed Chloe Flanders trundling along the concreted dockside wearing six inch stiletto heels that caused her generously proportioned chest to lean forwards. She almost fell over as she tried to wave, balance her voluptuous upper body and keep hold of her Gucci handbag.

Charles guffawed. "She reminds me of Barbara Windsor," he said loudly. The other bucket listers laughed, and Rachel agreed the scene was comical. Chloe eventually made it safely on board the second minibus with the assistance of the driver, who didn't even attempt to avert his gaze.

"I see we're not alone today," said Rachel. Is that group going to the same place?"

"Yes," answered Prudence. "There are two buses doing this tour. Georgia is escorting the rest of our party on a combined coach tour around the city along with a local tour guide."

The minibus engine lurched into life and the air conditioning started up, breathing some fresh, cool air into the rather hot bus. After a few minutes, the microphone came on, and Joe began a well-seasoned commentary, explaining some facts about Melbourne and describing points of interest as they passed them. Rachel paid attention as she had never visited the city before, but she did know it was the second most populous city in Australia and also the greenest.

Once the commentary stopped, Rachel turned to her travelling companion. "Deep, did you see the rather suave couple join the second minibus? I don't think they're part of your party."

"I didn't notice, but I think you will be referring to Harrison and Marion Scheffler. They are philanthropists, very wealthy. I think they made their money from mining in South Africa. They know a few of our South African friends – or should I say sons of our friends. Chloe invited them to join the tour yesterday after a mix-up with the bookings meant her group was undersubscribed. I think Charles knows them too."

"Who do I know?"

"Harrison and Marion," Deep answered.

"Ah yes, I have met them a couple of times. They seem to know a lot of people, so I can't remember who introduced us now. He's English, ex pat, and she's Saudi, I believe. They are very nice people, do a lot of good in the world – live in Mumbai now, I think, although they have residences around the globe."

Ideal for money laundering and moving antiquities around, then, thought Rachel as she nodded.

"Why did you ask?" Deep's penetrating gaze held her eyes.

"They seemed a little – how do I put this politely? – younger."

Deep laughed. "You're right, well below the average age of our little group. I think he's forty-one and she's roughly the same age. I read articles about them in the press from time to time."

Charles looked their way. "I think they're interested in buying Flanders's travel business now the mother's out of the way."

Deep stiffened in his seat and thrust his chin forward before picking up a book. Rachel patted his forearm.

Laughter from the front of the bus brought their concentration back as Joe started his commentary once more. They had driven past numerous colonial buildings dating back two centuries, and now they were in the countryside heading towards the first stop.

They were instructed to get off the bus at Dandenong National Park, home to giant eucalyptus trees. The trees formed a natural tunnel through which they walked before arriving in a tropical forest. Rachel was pleased to stretch her legs as she regretted not going for a run this morning. The group walked at a decent pace through the tunnel and this helped get rid of the cobwebs.

The forest was magnificent and just how she'd imagined Australian woodland to be, with enormous ferns and trees. The screeching sound of cockatoos flying over their heads grabbed their attention, the birds with their impressive head plumage clearly excited by their presence. Joe had explained they would be able to feed the parrots and cockatoos from a designated platform further along.

Once there, Rachel watched as the majority of the excited bunch became children again, revelling in a new experience. A small number of the group stayed well away from the platform, not wishing to get too close to the birds.

"I don't want bird poop landing on my head, thank you very much," she heard one of them remark.

The birds were exquisite to look at and it was wonderful to see them in the wild, not caged as they would be in the United Kingdom, although there were now parrots and parakeets living freely in and around London. Sarah had told her about this place, one of her favourites when she was given shore leave.

After feeding the relatively tame birds for a while, they had to make way for the second group that included the Schefflers. Harrison Scheffler was a tall, heavyset man with tanned skin and light green keenly focussed eyes. He was casually dressed in khaki knee-length shorts and a brown t-shirt. His wife was beautiful: olive skinned, slim, with long shiny black hair tied in a ponytail, wearing mid-thigh denim shorts and a yellow vest.

In spite of their casual dress, the couple oozed opulence and everything about them shrieked designer, from the clothes to the elaborate jewellery adorning both of them. Rachel's eye was drawn to an unusual black stone worn around Marion's neck. Moon shaped, it was around four inches in length and the thick gold chain holding it in place suggested its weight.

The couple were engrossed in conversation with Chloe, Joe's wife, who was struggling to walk through the forest in her ridiculous heels. Harrison Scheffler nodded towards Charles as they passed in the opposite direction. Patty bumped into him and looked mortified, but he shrugged it off politely and helped her pick up her handbag, handing it back to her before Emma could scold the poor woman. Rachel wished she was part of the other group so that she could do what Robert's group clearly weren't able to do at present, for whatever reason.

Deep was waiting for her as she had slowed to a snail's pace.

"Why are you interested in the Schefflers?"

Realising she was being too obvious, she kicked herself. "I was fascinated by the necklace Mrs Scheffler was wearing, it is so beautiful. I don't think I've ever seen a stone like it."

"Can't say I noticed. Anyway, young lady, you need to be careful. Sometimes it's best to stay out of other people's business."

Was that a concerned warning or a threat warning? "Don't worry about me, Deep. I guess I'm fascinated by the rich and glamorous."

Deep didn't look convinced, but didn't say anything further. He held out his arm for her to take and she did so. Within minutes they had caught up with the group and were boarding a steam train for a ride through the rain forest.

The steam train ride was magnificent and the beautiful scenery managed to take Rachel's mind off the strange couple and their presence on the other bus. They hadn't spoken to anyone in particular while Rachel was watching, so perhaps they really were just catching up with old friends.

The rest of the day passed by unremarkably. Glenis insisted on Rachel staying with them and didn't allow her to stray again. The second minibus passengers followed their own guide, Chloe, or perhaps it was the other way around as Chloe's chest and the stilettos were not designed for this kind of outing. Rachel realised that Florence Flanders would have most likely been the designated guide for one of the buses before her unfortunate demise. She chuckled to herself as she imagined Joe cancelling Chloe's beauty salon appointments and putting her in his mother's place.

The party ate lunch in the park before leaving for the Yarra River Valley and a visit to one of the wineries. Rachel tasted an exquisite full-bodied, spicy Shiraz, and then they were taken to a dairy farm to sample local soft cheeses.

Deep and Glenis fell asleep on the way back, but Charles was as alert as ever, as was the caustic Emma who managed to say something negative about every stop. Patty seemed blissfully oblivious to her companion's sour tongue, nodding and smiling happily.

"Did you enjoy the day, Rachel?" asked Prudence, who was still sitting directly behind her. Deep had opted for the window seat and was snoring quietly.

"I did, I can't thank you enough for including me. I would never have done a tour like this if I'd been left to my own devices."

Nor would I have been able to afford it, she thought.

"Oh, don't give it another thought. It was a pleasure to have you. I did so enjoy the winery."

"It would have been better if we could have spent more time there," interrupted Emma from her seat diagonally opposite.

Yes so you could have knocked back more free wine.

Rachel was annoyed with herself for allowing the woman to get under her skin, but she couldn't help noticing Emma's behaviour at the winery, sneakily drinking her own and Patty's wine, and then Rachel had been disgusted to see her emptying the glasses of some of the party who hadn't finished their drinks.

"It was good, but I liked the dairy farm too," Prudence answered. "It's a shame we couldn't have had the cheese at the same time as the wine."

"I'm not much of a one for cheese," said Emma. "The place reeked if you ask me."

"We didn't," growled Rachel under her breath.

Thankfully Charles intervened before Emma could go off on yet another negative tirade.

"I was only in Melbourne last year, but today has been most pleasant."

"This is supposed to be a bucket list tour, Charles," Prudence admonished. "So far, you've been to every place we've visited."

Charles's eyes darted around quickly before he answered. "Yes, well, I've never cruised before."

"Hmm, well you seem to know a lot about it for someone who has never been on one before." Prudence narrowed her eyes as she looked at the man opposite Rachel. Rachel saw the redness extending from his neck up his face.

Why would he lie about something like that? Surely he's not involved in anything shady.

Rachel turned back into her seat to look out of the window as thoughts whirred round in her head.

Chapter 24

They arrived back at port at 5pm. The minibus pulled up on the dockside where the magnificent *Coral Queen* was moored in all her glory. Passengers were walking hurriedly back up the steps on to the ship. The sun rained down a bright glow, capturing the luxury vessel as though setting her up for a grand photo opportunity.

Rachel stretched her legs and turned to Glenis, whom she assisted from the bus while the driver was gratefully accepting tips from the wealthy group.

"Thank you so much for a lovely day. I'm just going to take a walk along the dockside before getting back on board."

Glenis answered, yawning, tired after a long day, "It was a pleasure to have you along, Rachel. Will we see you at dinner?"

"I hope so, see you later."

Rachel turned away from the ship and walked as far as she could within the confines of the area cordoned off by security. There wasn't much to see other than cargo vessels further along, although there was another cruise ship leaving the opposite side of the port. She watched for a while as it moved away from the dock and floated slowly out to sea.

Time to get back to the Coral before it too sets sail.

She turned around and walked back towards the ship. With most passengers already on board, she noticed a police car which hadn't been parked there when her minibus had returned. To her surprise, two policemen walked down the steps from the ship with Robert, whose hands were handcuffed in front of him. Their eyes met briefly, the resignation clearly visible in his as he was led towards the waiting police car.

She stood frozen for what seemed like an age, watching helplessly as the police car drove through the port barriers. The sun had gone in as if to accentuate the confusion and fear she felt for Robert being arrested in a country so far away from home. The cold made her shiver, or was it the memories of happier times, now completely destroyed?

"Ma'am?" A crewman wearing grey overalls called to her. She looked at his weather-worn face, noticing the nicotine-stained teeth as he smiled at her, but she didn't move. "Ma'am, the ship's leaving in twenty minutes. We're pulling up the steps. Please board, ma'am."

She looked back towards the road where Robert had been driven away and pondered going after him, but she had no idea where the police had taken him. To the police station, she presumed. The utter confusion that coursed through her veins made her legs turn to jelly. She couldn't move and tears stung the back of her eyes as she felt her legs give way and the world turned black.

"Rachel?" Sarah's voice broke through the gloom and she found herself lying on a stretcher being wheeled towards the all-too-familiar infirmary on deck two. "Rachel, are you okay?"

Her eyes opened and she saw Sarah's concerned face alongside the wheeled stretcher. Waverley's equally worried expression was on the other side.

"I'm sorry, I think I fainted."

"You did," said Waverley. "Thankfully a crewman caught you before you collapsed on to the concrete."

"Oh, please thank him for me. I think he was trying to encourage me to get back on board just before everything went black."

By now they had arrived in the infirmary and Bernard was checking her blood pressure while putting a probe on her index finger to check her oxygen levels. Leads were attached to her chest and a monitor showed her heart rate was faster than normal at ninety-eight beats per minute. Dr Bentley arrived and dismissed everyone but Sarah while he examined her.

"I feel better now." Rachel tried to sit up but still felt slightly weak. Her heart rate was gradually falling back down to her usual sixty-four.

"It was just a faint," said Dr Bentley. "You'll feel better after something to eat and drink, and then we'll discharge you. Just for once, I would like you to be on board ship and not land up in my infirmary." He opened the curtains that protected her privacy and she was pleased to see the happy faces of the medical team. Even Waverley laughed at Dr Bentley's joke.

"Believe it or not, I'd like that too."

"Rachel, may I have a word?" Waverley coughed as he often did when he had either bad or sensitive news.

"Yes, of course."

Raggie arrived with a tray of tea and biscuits and Waverley sat down at the bedside. Rachel sat up, noticing that most of the team had left as it was time for evening surgery. Sarah remained and took a seat on the opposite side of the bed.

"The lady you both found yesterday is in an induced coma to allow the swelling in the brain time to go down. The doctors are not sure if she will recover, and if she does, whether she will have any memory of the events that took place yesterday."

"That is tragic." Rachel picked at the bed sheet and noticed Sarah chewing her bottom lip, which meant there was worse to come.

"Erm, that's not all. Mr Chowdry has accused a Mr Robert Hutchins of attempted murder." He coughed and looked at Sarah before continuing. "I understand you know… erm knew Mr Hutchins?"

The tears stung the back of her eyes again, the trembling returned and she felt her lips go dry. She reached over and took a sip of the tea.

"We were engaged once, so yes, I did know him. He is not capable of doing this; he can be controlling, obstinate and a pain in the neck, but he is not a murderer." Her voice sounded loud and distant, as if not belonging to her, and she noticed her heart rate had risen again, but this time she inhaled a few slow, deep breaths before continuing. "Is there any evidence against him?"

"They have her mobile phone which apparently reveals that she and," he coughed again, "Mr Hutchins were having an affair."

"I knew about that. Sarah and I spoke with him last night." She didn't mention his admitting to removing evidence from a crime scene. "That doesn't prove he attacked her. Surely her husband is the chief suspect, crime of passion and all that?"

"That would be the case, but Mr Chowdry has a cast-iron alibi for the time of the attack. He was with a lady from the bucket list tour, chatting about the wildlife they had both seen apparently."

"Oh, I see. But there must be more than the fact they were having an affair for them to arrest him?"

"You know about the arrest then? I did wonder if that's what had caused you to pass out. I'm so sorry, Rachel." Sarah took her hand and squeezed it.

"His fingerprints were all over the place." Waverley looked at Rachel as if gauging her reaction. Surely he couldn't think she had had anything to do with it? She hoped Sarah hadn't given him details of last night's conversation with Robert.

"I still don't believe he attacked her."

"Then why would his fingerprints be everywhere? The paramedics confirmed he wasn't allowed to touch her once you arrived on scene. Sarah's prints were also there, but we know why that was. Rachel, I'm sorry, but you have to admit the evidence is compelling. People change; perhaps he's not the man you thought he was and perhaps you had a lucky escape."

She exchanged a glance with Sarah, who shook her head. "I don't know why his prints are there, but there's something else going on, I'm sure."

Waverley stiffened. "And what might that be?"

Rachel looked down. "I don't know."

Seeing her twirling the engagement ring on her finger, Waverley softened his tone once more. "Congratulations, I see you and Carlos have finally agreed to tie the knot."

She felt her face flushing and the happiness returning at the mention of Carlos. "Yes, just before this cruise."

"Then I suggest you forget about this incident. Sarah informs me that you hadn't seen this man for a couple of years. If he's innocent, a lawyer will be able to prove it, and if he's guilty, he deserves everything he gets." Waverley stood. "Take it from me, marriage is wonderful." He bounced out of the infirmary with a huge grin on his face.

"Thanks for not telling him about the evidence tampering, but we might have to if we don't find out what's going on."

"I almost did, to be honest. I was worried about how he'd react, but I also didn't want to blow Robert's investigation, although I'm not sure how much of an operation will be left now."

"That reminds me, the couple Robert's team have been following were on the second minibus on our tour today. Apparently they know the South African group. Deep says they are well-known philanthropists, Harrison and Marion Scheffler, and Charles also knows them a little. I'm going to look them up – I'll buy an internet pass later.

"Sarah, I know you don't like Robert, and he's not my favourite person in the world either, but he didn't do this. If it wasn't Sunita's husband, it must have something to do with that couple, the Schefflers, part of whatever it is they're up to."

"Before I get involved any further, can I ask you something?"

"Anything."

"Are you still in love with Robert? And if so, what about Carlos?"

"That's two questions." Rachel caressed her engagement ring. "I admit I was thrown when I bumped into him again and I have done some deep heart searching over the past few days. The thing is, I was in love with the memories of Robert, of our first year together and the promise of our successful future. Since I've met him again, although those old memories have stirred, they don't reach my heart in the same way that Carlos does. The relationship with Carlos is based on a much more solid foundation – not only do I love him, I respect him. I can be myself with him. I never felt that way about Robert, and I was certainly not allowed to be myself with him, he was far too critical and controlling. When he broke off our engagement a part of me died inside, a part that I'm still struggling to resurrect so that I can give myself to Carlos, knowing I'm holding nothing back. But I'm not there yet."

Sarah nodded. "I think that's where Jason's at, so I do understand where you're coming from, but let me tell you something, Rachel Prince, from the other side. It sucks. I long for the day when Jason lets go of whatever pain that woman caused him and, believe it or not, I bet Carlos longs for the day you let go too. The very fact he's given you so much time speaks volumes; he was smitten with you the day you met. You have to believe it's possible, Rachel, or it will hold you both back for years to come. Trust me, I know."

Sarah hugged Rachel and they held on to each other for a long moment as only best friends who have bared their souls can do. Tears fell down Rachel's cheeks.

"It will happen for all of us, I promise."

They drank tea in comfortable silence for a few minutes while they both composed themselves again before deciding on the next plan of action. Rachel had no idea how she was going to prove Robert's innocence or find Mrs F's murderer, but she was going to get to the bottom of both cases over the next few sea days. If need be, she and Sarah would have to tell Waverley about their conversation with Robert the previous evening, but for now that would remain untold.

"I wonder if Robert's room has been searched?" she said.

"I would have thought it likely, seeing as the police came aboard to arrest him."

"They weren't carrying anything when they left, neither was Robert. Can you find out if he has a roommate?"

Sarah crossed the infirmary to the computer and pulled up the passenger records.

Rachel was discharged from the infirmary when Dr Bentley came in after surgery.

"I'm going to my room to wash and change," she said to Sarah. "Shall we meet in the buffet in an hour?"

"An hour sounds great. I need to meet with Bernard to take the on-call bag, I'm on tonight."

Minutes later, Rachel unlocked her room with the key card and noticed an envelope had been pushed under the door. Picking it up and recognising the handwriting, she ripped it open and hurried over to the sitting area.

"Rachel, by now I will have been arrested. I saw the police boarding from my balcony and don't have long to write this. I know they're coming for me. I've called the team who are on land and explained they may have to abandon the mission.

"You have to believe me when I say that I did not attack Sunita. I would never hit a woman, no matter what you think of me. My freedom depends on you now."

Rachel read that part again and gasped at the enormity of the task in hand. After pouring herself a whiskey shot from the fully stocked fridge, she sat down and picked up the letter again. The whiskey burned the back of her throat – not her drink of choice, but the effects helped her fix her attention back on the letter.

"I've suspected since early on in the mission that we had a mole in the team – the couple we are following always seem to be one step ahead, and after you suggested last night that the hunter had become the hunted, I realised you were right, even though I was too pig-headed to believe it at the time. Someone knows who the ringleader is and has given us up. Clearly I can't warn the team because I don't know who to trust!

"Take this letter to whoever is responsible for security on board the ship and tell him to contact my boss on the number at the top. Tell him my case notes are in the safe – you'll know the passcode.

Try to stay out of it yourself, it's too dangerous, but if security won't listen, do whatever you have to. Be careful, Rachel. Trust no-one.

"Best, Robert."

This brought with it a whole new slant to the case. Her first reaction was to take the letter directly to Waverley, but would he listen to her? He'd already decided Robert was guilty and would see this as a ploy to draw attention away from his guilt. Then she would have to come clean about knowing that Robert had removed evidence from the crime scene. Waverley would be angry and likely to come to the conclusion that she was being played by Robert, a conclusion that she herself hadn't completely ruled out.

No, she would go ahead with her evening plans and see where that led to first. If she didn't get anywhere, Waverley would be the first to know.

There was barely time to shower and change before she met up with Sarah. Glenis would be annoyed at her for not joining the group for dinner, but she could live with that.

Chapter 25

A Maori theme was taking place in the buffet this evening with traditional dishes rising to the challenge. The world-class chefs on board never disappointed, and tonight was no exception, with time-honoured dishes consisting of fish and sweet potatoes.

"You're on time for a change." Sarah appeared behind Rachel with a tray laden with food.

Rachel laughed at the size of the meal. "I take it you're hungry."

"I've told you before, when I'm on call I never know when I'll get to eat again. Bernard and I live by the 'it's always best to stock up' side of the argument, whereas Brigitte and Gwen live by the 'I don't mind if I disappear' side." Both women laughed as they sought a table in the relatively quiet buffet.

"You never seem to gain weight, though."

"Neither would you if you ran up and down this ship like I do!"

While they ate, they chatted about trivial matters, but after allowing Sarah to eat in peace, Rachel produced the letter and handed it to her friend. Sarah's face turned serious as she read through it.

"We have to take this to Waverley."

Rachel had anticipated this reaction as Sarah would always veer towards keeping her safe. "After what he said this afternoon, I'm not sure he'll believe it. He will just assume that Robert is using me."

"An opinion I'm likely to agree with," Sarah said loudly.

"That's my point. If you feel that way, how much more is Waverley going to? Look, I'm not saying we don't take it to Waverley, but let's go ahead with our plan first. We'll check out Robert's room, pull his case notes, and then, if there's nothing useful in them, go to the chief. I'm not stupid, Sarah, I know this could be a ruse, but let's just give him the benefit of the doubt for old times' sake. Besides, he looked desperate when I saw the police taking him away, and if there is a mole, we don't want to alert them."

"Who might the mole be?"

"That, my dear friend, is what we're going to find out."

Sarah sighed. "Come on then, now's as good a time as any. The stateroom stewards should have finished their evening rounds and guests will most likely be out and about. I have my uniform on and the on-call bag, so anyone seeing us will assume we're on official business."

The two women made their way downstairs to deck seven and found Robert's room at the stern. Sarah used her universal key card to open the door, after looking up and down the corridor to check no-one would notice. A young couple were visible at the far end, but looked like dots in the distance, the corridors were so long.

They entered the room and Sarah used her card for the lights. The bed had not been turned down; the steward had likely been told to leave the room as it was. The stateroom was similar to Rachel's with a queen-sized bed, chairs and a bed settee. She took a deep breath, trying not to imagine Robert languishing in a custody cell in an Australian police station. Crooked cops were not given an easy time by the police or criminals, so he had a difficult few days ahead of him, with much worse waiting for him if he was transferred to a prison.

"Hurry up, Rachel, we can't be found in here."

Rachel looked around at the messy room and her heart sank. "We're too late."

Sarah also took in the room's state. "It's been ransacked! We have to call Waverley now."

Rachel walked towards the cupboard housing the safe. The door was ajar and the safe was empty.

"I agree, we also need to get out of here. The room could be being watched. I just hope Robert didn't leave any information about me in here." She swallowed hard, thinking back to the first few days on board and how Robert had openly approached her. Bragging rights would have been irresistible to him and whoever did this must surely know about their prior relationship. She just had to hope they wouldn't suspect her of being involved in an investigation. Robert had been very discreet when he'd met with her and Sarah the other night, so she hoped he wasn't being watched then and that her initial rejection of her old flame had told the mole there was nothing to worry about as far as she was concerned.

"Check the corridor, Sarah."

"Rachel, you're frightening me. What's going on?"

"Nothing, we just don't want to come under a desperate gang's radar, that's all."

Sarah nodded and looked through the spy hole. "It's clear opposite."

Rachel opened the door slowly and checked the corridor. An older man was going into his room about halfway down.

Once he'd gone, she whispered, "Clear." With a pounding heart and anxiety building, she waited for Sarah to remove her card from the lights and close the door quietly. They walked hastily towards midships. Every person they passed looked suspicious to Rachel in her heightened state of alertness.

"Rachel, we missed you at dinner." Glenis exited as they arrived in front of the six passenger lifts that ran up and down the ship.

"Sorry, I decided to have a light meal for a change and meet up with Sarah."

The older woman's eyes narrowed as she looked at Sarah, who was slightly out of breath from pulling the heavy on-call bag behind her at the pace Rachel had set.

"I didn't know you were on this floor?"

"I'm not. Sarah was called to see someone so I've been waiting here for her. Come on, Sarah, you promised me a drink."

"You girls have fun. See you tomorrow, Rachel. I think we're going to need that self-defence." Glenis turned the corner to follow the corridor down the way they had just come.

"That was close," said Sarah. "What did she mean by that?"

"No idea, but let's get out of here before any of the other bucket listers come along. I didn't realise they were on this deck either. It's all a bit too much of a coincidence for my liking."

"What does that mean? Surely you can't think any of them would be involved in this smuggling business?"

Rachel giggled. "Not really, but stranger things have happened. I would like to know how many of them have cruised before. Joe Flanders is also in the ideal position for a smuggling operation, don't you think? Is he on this floor too?"

Sarah frowned. "Yes he is. I don't want to be rude, but he just doesn't seem intelligent enough."

"What about the new model wife? Or even the daughter?"

"No, I can't believe Georgia is involved. Besides, she was drugged, remember?"

An uneasy feeling occurred to Rachel, one she wasn't yet prepared to share with Sarah.

They were getting out of the lifts on deck nine when Sarah's radio went off. "Accident deck twelve, passenger slipped by the main pool."

Sarah sighed heavily. "I'd better go. Rachel, you need to take that letter to Waverley so that he'll at least go and look in Robert's room, which will add reasonable doubt to his guilt."

Rachel shrugged. "Unless he says Robert did all that before he left to make it look like a burglary," she muttered under her breath as Sarah dashed back towards the lifts. "This case is getting more and more complicated."

After standing in the corridor for some time and giving herself a good talking to, she finally decided to turn around and follow Sarah's advice and go to see Waverley. How much she would be telling him would be firmly in his court.

Deck three, where the chief of security's office could be found, was quiet. Half hoping the office would be in darkness, Rachel was disappointed to see the lights on and the blinds open. Waverley, Jason and a few other officers including Ravanos, an officer she'd met previously, were engaged in a meeting, probably a handover or catch up. For all she knew they could be looking at wedding photos.

Perhaps it's best not to disturb them, she thought, but before she could about-turn, Waverley spotted her and waved her in. At least he was smiling.

"Miss Prince."

Oh, we're back to that, are we? "Chief Waverley," she returned, but then smiled, knowing she shouldn't start this off on the wrong foot. "May I have a word?"

He frowned as she looked towards the other officers, wanting him to dismiss them. "Okay, boys, off you go. Goodridge, you stay, I need to speak to you."

Rachel didn't mind Jason staying because he was on her side. Robert's letter had said to trust no-one, and if the criminals could infiltrate his team, they could certainly infiltrate cruise ship security, so she didn't want anyone else present for now.

"Take a seat, Rachel." Waverley gestured towards the two armchairs and sofa circling a coffee table.

After they were all seated, Rachel on one armchair, Jason on the other and Waverley on the sofa, she spoke. "I have something to show you." She handed over the letter from Robert. Waverley picked it up and scrutinised the document before passing it on for Jason to read.

"I suppose you believe he's telling the truth?" Waverley sounded sceptical.

"Almost one hundred per cent, but I have considered it might be a ruse to get you to look into his case."

"I'm happy to hear you've considered it at least, although it does have an element of truth. I think you had better tell us what you know about the case he's working on."

"I don't know a great deal actually. He appeared at our table last night while I was having a drink with Sarah. I had already worked out he was following a couple who I now know to be Harrison and Marion Scheffler." Waverley shifted uncomfortably in his seat, but said nothing so Rachel continued. "He said his team was investigating an international money laundering and artefact smuggling ring. He confessed to having an affair with Sunita Chowdry, maintaining he hadn't taken his eye off the ball, but they hadn't managed to find much out. I suggested he had been rumbled as you can see from the letter, but he didn't agree at the time. Now it seems he does, and suspects that this might have something to do with the attack on his colleague… erm, girlfriend."

"And if it weren't for the fact her husband has a concrete alibi, he would be the more likely suspect for the attack on Mrs Chowdry. I'm not falling for the whole story, but let's say Hutchins is telling the truth and he is innocent – do you think one of the Schefflers attacked Mrs Chowdry? They are very important people, we wouldn't want to approach them without concrete proof."

"It could have been one or both of them, they were certainly on the same tour, but it could also have been the ringleader of this smuggling racket, whoever that might be. I can't see it being a stranger, and the attacker must have known about the affair because of the evidence—"

Blast! She had let the cat out of the bag now.

Waverley's eyes narrowed as he stared intensely at her. "What evidence?"

"Robert found some of his own things at the crime scene and he suspected he was being framed so he, erm, removed them," she answered quietly, unable to hold Waverley's gaze as the guilt of hiding this from him surfaced.

"And when, might I ask, were you going to tell me about this?"

Rachel couldn't answer because she wasn't sure whether she would have told him at all if it hadn't slipped out or if Robert hadn't been arrested. Waverley looked at Jason and shook his head. Jason looked disappointed, clearly knowing that Sarah had also hidden the information from them.

"I don't think we can do anything about that now, sir. Perhaps we should take a look in Mr Hutchins's room?"

Waverley stood up and straightened his uniform. He had gained a few pounds since Rachel had last seen him, and as his new wife was a senior baker, he was unlikely to lose weight anytime soon.

"Are you coming with us?"

"Erm, no. I think I'll go to bed if that's alright? I'm tired." Rachel couldn't face hiding any more information from the chief of security, but she couldn't admit that she and Sarah had already been in the room and there was nothing to find.

"Mm, I'm pleased to see you're leaving it to us after all. What passcode is Hutchins referring to in the letter?"

"2014, the year he became a sergeant."

"Thanks. We'll call his boss after we've gone through the room.

"Well, goodnight, Rachel. Perhaps we can meet up in the morning to go through this in more detail. Please bring Sarah Bradshaw along with you." It was a command rather than a request, so Rachel nodded.

"We could come at lunchtime. Sarah will have surgery and is on call tonight so I don't want to wake her early, and I have a self-defence class to teach until eleven-thirty."

"Make it two o'clock then. That will give Sarah time to eat."

Rachel nodded and briskly left the office, hoping against hope that Waverley wouldn't suspect that she had already checked Robert's room. She had no doubt that Jason would, but when push came to shove, she knew he would protect Sarah. She sighed heavily, feeling like the world was upon her shoulders and deeply regretting her evening soirée.

As she made her way back towards her room, she couldn't help thinking she was missing something that was staring her in the face. It wouldn't come to her, whatever it was, and her brain was already in overdrive with all the events of the past few days.

Her room was dark when she arrived, but a sense of foreboding gripped her. Her hands shook as she placed the card in the lighting slot and the dim lights came on. Walking boldly but slowly along the corridor into the main part of the room, she felt a hand close over her mouth.

"I'm not going to hurt you – tell me you won't do anything stupid and I'll let you go."

Rachel didn't recognise the voice, but nodded and her assailant did let her go, pushing her ahead of him to allow room for escape if he needed it. Her heart was still pumping twenty to the dozen so she didn't say anything immediately.

"I'm sorry. I had to know if Rob left you anything."

Rachel recognised the man as Jack Chowdry, Sunita's husband.

"Why are you here, and more importantly how did you get in?" Her heart was slowing up a little, although she could still feel tremors in her hands and her throat was parched. She poured herself a glass of water.

They both stood, weighing each other up like lions deciding whether to get into a fight.

"I managed to borrow a card from the steward's trolley while she was distracted by another passenger. I put it back before she realised it had moved after jamming your door open. I need to know if Rob attacked Sunita. I know about the affair."

Chowdry's eyes welled up and he looked down at the floor. Having been on the receiving end of Robert's roving eye, she softened.

"As you're here, you might as well have a drink. What can I get you?"

His shoulders hunched and he relaxed, flopping on to one of the armchairs.

"Scotch."

Rachel poured a scotch for him and a brandy for herself and took the settee opposite. "Robert told me he didn't attack your wife. You'll be pleased to know he didn't think you could have done it either." It felt better not to mention the removal of evidence as this could only make matters worse.

Chowdry sighed. "I thought he was my friend."

And I thought he was my fiancé when he wandered off, she wanted to say, but didn't.

"May I ask why you're not with your wife?"

"She's plugged into a thousand machines, while the attacker, if it isn't Rob, is still on board this ship. I needed to do something – I'm no good at sitting around, not to mention being angry. I wasn't the right person to be sitting there with her. I called her sister yesterday, she lives in Chennai. She arrived this morning and sent me away to find out who did this."

"Does she know about the affair?"

"Not yet, but I'm sure she will soon enough if the police turn up at the hospital again."

"They've arrested Robert, but I guess you knew that."

"I insisted upon it once I found the text messages. He deserves that at least." Chowdry spat the words out.

"Who do you think attacked your wife?"

"If it wasn't Rob, and it certainly wasn't me, then it has to be a couple we've been tracking."

"Are they prone to violence?"

"Not that we know of, but they are slippery characters, always managing to evade detection. We do have a video of them now, bringing contraband into the country – an informer gave it to us in return for a lesser sentence. That started the ball rolling for Operation Cruise Ship."

Rachel's eyebrows hit the ceiling – *seriously*? "So what have you found out?"

"Absolutely nothing. They haven't taken a step out of line – no secret meetings, no nothing."

"Perhaps they are just on holiday. I presume you don't want me to know who this couple is and I don't really want to know." *Trust no-one!* Robert's words screamed in her head before she gave anything away. "I don't know anything else so I can't help you, I'm afraid. I wouldn't know this much if Robert hadn't insisted on declaring his innocence, and to be quite honest with you, I'm not sure whether to believe him or not. That's for the courts to decide."

"So you're not going to help me find out who did this to my wife?"

"Even if I wanted to, I couldn't. It's nothing to do with me. Besides, Robert and I ended things a long time ago."

Chowdry sighed, almost with relief, Rachel thought. "You're right, and it could be dangerous for you to be involved."

Rachel was thoughtful for a moment. "Why don't you go and see the chief of security? Perhaps he can help."

"I'll think about it. Look, I'm sorry again for breaking into your room; I just needed to know if he was guilty or not. You should be careful, though, because if the couple we're following get a sniff of your past relationship with Rob, they might want to do something about you too."

"I don't have any interest in them so I don't see that as likely."

Chowdry rose to leave but Rachel stopped him with a question.

"By the way, how did you know what room I was in?"

"We were given a full passenger manifest by the border force on boarding day. I'm in charge of IT so it was easy to track you down."

"Did Robert have access to that list?"

"Yes, why?"

"Just curious to know how many other people are invading my privacy, that's all."

Chowdry smiled. "Don't worry, it wasn't you we were interested in."

Chowdry left and Rachel fell back on to the settee with more questions than answers. What was that really all about? Did he think she was in danger or was he worried Robert had told her something?

As she finished her drink, she stared into space. This case was far more complicated than anything she had come across before. So many lies, the suspect list was increasing, and all the time there was still the feeling that something obvious was just beyond her grasp.

Chapter 26

Following a fitful night's sleep, Rachel woke early and did what she always did when things got to her: she ran. The run around the track on deck sixteen cleared some of the cobwebs away and at least enabled her to narrow her suspect list down to fewer than ten.

There was still the murder of poor Mrs F to consider, as the late woman no longer seemed to be a priority on anyone's radar other than Deep's. It was time to find out a little more about Joe and Chloe Flanders and rule them in or out of the frame for the murder. If they were not responsible, the murderer had to be one of the bucket list party, so with renewed vigour, Rachel intended to find out who it was.

After returning to her room to shower and change, she called Sarah to let her know about their summons to Waverley's office.

"That's all I need. Now Jason will be annoyed with me – again – and I've hardly slept. Half the ship seemed to have accidents last night, including the crew!"

"Any from the bucket list?"

"No. Did I tell you, Bernard's started calling them the *wellderly* because they're never ill? He read the word somewhere and it's become his new favourite."

Rachel laughed. "They most certainly are well. Many of them remind me of Marjorie, she's as spritely as ever. I do hope I'm as fit as they are when I get to their age."

"With the amount of exercise you do, Rachel, you'll probably be fitter – not to mention you hardly touch fat!"

"I'm one of the lucky ones, I don't really like unhealthy food, except for the odd fat burst. Maybe I'll have a drink problem instead if I keep hitting the spirits. Speaking of which, tell Bernard not to give any of the wellderly a stinger or they won't be well for very long."

Rachel chuckled at her own joke. Bernard's stinger cocktail was a notoriously potent drink and the recipe his closely guarded secret.

"No fear of that happening, Gwen would give him a fortnight's on calls if he did such a thing. What do you mean, if you keep hitting the spirits?"

"It's a long story, I'll tell you about it later. For now, I'd better head to my class, where I'll see a crowd of wellderly!"

The self-defence class passed without mishap, and it seemed even Emma was beginning to thaw towards Rachel. She was by no means friendly, but at least she was more polite, firing the barbs she usually reserved for Rachel towards Charles instead. He just let them wash over his head. Glenis, however, was acting strangely; she was almost distant.

Perhaps the wellderly go through a second adolescence.

Rachel didn't have time for moody games; she had enough on her plate and was dreading the meeting with Waverley, who by now would know that Robert's room had been ransacked. The fine line between truth and lies was nagging at her conscience. Her father had always taught her to tell the truth no matter what the consequences, but then, he had not been in the police force or tried to track down criminals.

"Will you join us for lunch?" Prudence asked Rachel after the class finished.

"I can't today, sorry. I'm meeting my friend."

"Come along, Pru, we need to get on," Glenis called impatiently. Rachel waved, but Glenis stormed off, leaving her waving at the air.

Awkward, she thought. *I must catch up with Glenis later and find out what's wrong with her.*

After packing away the laptop and a few exercise mats that hadn't been used, she made her way downstairs to the buffet. Sarah was already there with Bernard, Gwen and Brigitte. The bright white uniforms stood out a mile.

Rachel filled a plate with food and joined them.

"Hello there, Rachel," said Gwen, smiling. "Have you tracked down our killer yet?" she asked, lowering her voice.

"Not yet, I thought I'd have lunch first," Rachel answered cheekily.

"The killer's a bit slippery, eh?" Bernard joked, clearly referring to the earlier snake incident.

"I do wish you lot would not joke about such things. One, I don't like snakes, and secondly, I do not like murderers roaming around on board my ship," said Brigitte.

"*Your* ship?" Sarah nudged the French nurse.

"You know what I mean."

"I don't know what your problem is," said Bernard. "There are only two murderers – two out of three-and-a-half thousand is not that many." He sat back in his chair, challenging Brigitte to more banter.

"You wouldn't find it so funny if you were the target," she retorted. "Anyway, there is also eighteen hundred crew on board this ship, for your information."

"I think Bernard was referring to the passengers, Brigitte. Anyway, Bernard, cut the teasing. You know we're sensitive about these things."

Gwen put her arm around Brigitte. Bernard opened his mouth, but thought better of it, although Rachel was sure Gwen was not as sensitive as Brigitte.

"Did Dr Bentley's family join him in Melbourne? I forgot to ask."

"Yes," answered Sarah. "He's over the moon. They are doing a tour of the ship as we speak, and tonight they join the captain's table for dinner. That always goes down well."

"I feel sorry for Captain Jenson, always being on show – sold to the highest bidder," said Bernard.

"Well don't, he loves it. Anyway it's par for the course if you want to head up a cruise ship," said Gwen. "In fact Graham's invited me to join them tonight."

Was that a blush? Now she came to think of it, Gwen and Dr Bentley would make an ideal couple, but perhaps he was just being friendly, and as neither seemed keen to be in a relationship, a budding romance was unlikely.

"Ooooh," said Bernard, echoing her own thoughts, but Sarah's kick under the table stopped him in his tracks so he moved off topic. "Anyway, I'd love to stay and chat, but I'm on call. Ciao."

Gwen and Brigitte left soon afterwards, then Sarah turned serious.

"I feel like I'm heading into a storm."

"You and me, both," agreed Rachel. "There's one forecast for later. Come on, let's get it over with."

Waverley was alone when they arrived, resulting in Sarah visibly relaxing at not having to face Jason. Rachel knew she would prefer to have *that* conversation privately. He summoned them inside with a wave, but appeared flustered, searching around his desk for something.

The two women glanced at each other and stood, waiting to be invited to sit.

"Ah, here it is." He lifted up a folder triumphantly. "I can't seem to get back in gear just yet. Strictly speaking, I'm still on honeymoon. Anyway, you two don't want to hear about that. Take a seat. Coffee?"

He was more chipper than Rachel had expected. *These mood swings are catching.*

"Yes please," answered Sarah.

Waverley picked up the telephone and ordered a pot of freshly ground coffee, then he joined them around the table.

"Right, there have been some developments since last night." That explained his bouncy demeanour. Rachel thought this might let her and Sarah off the hook.

"Really?" she answered. "Good news, I take it?"

"Mostly good, but I'll start with the bad. After you left last night, Goodridge and I went to Mr Hutchins's room, but unfortunately someone had been there before us."

"Oh," was all Rachel could say, and Sarah tried badly to feign surprise.

"You can cut the pretence, ladies. We have security footage from the corridor."

"Oh," Rachel repeated, this time with an embarrassed intonation. "You don't seem angry."

"I'm not, although I do wish you wouldn't lead our crew members astray." He smiled encouragingly at Sarah, and Rachel sighed with relief. At least she hadn't got her friend in trouble.

The meeting was interrupted momentarily as a pot of coffee was delivered from the kitchen. Waverley poured them each a drink.

"So what else did the footage reveal?" asked Rachel.

"We looked at all movements along the corridor over the past few days. As you would expect, there were a lot of tedious comings and goings. The bucket list tour group are staying on that floor too, so there are times when the corridor is crowded with them and their paraphernalia."

Rachel assumed he meant walking aids or wheelchairs as some of them did require assistance.

"Did anyone unusual go into Robert's room?"

"Just thirty minutes before you two ventured in, a man was seen leaving, so we reversed the footage. He went in with empty hands and came out fifteen minutes later carrying a briefcase."

"Who was he?" asked Sarah.

Waverley pushed the folder towards them.

"Chowdry," said Rachel before opening it.

"How did you know that?" Waverley's bubble had burst.

"Because he also broke into my room last night. He was waiting for me when I got back, scared the life out of me, but said he just wanted to know whether Robert had told me anything and to gauge whether I thought he had attacked his wife."

"You should have called me, Rachel. We can't have people roaming around the ship breaking into guest rooms."

"Sorry."

"So you should be, Rachel Prince. Now you might be in danger too. How did he even know what room you were in?" asked Sarah.

"Apparently he and Robert were given a copy of the ship's guests along with room numbers. They have it on a computer file, something to do with their case."

Waverley looked furious but held his peace.

"I don't think he's our murderer, though. There's no link between him and Mrs Flanders. Perhaps he also suspects there's a mole."

"He does," said Waverley. "We have questioned him at length and I agree with you. I don't think he's the culprit, but we will watch him nonetheless. I've let him go for now so that he can carry on working with his colleagues and see if he can find out what the heck's going on. There is something else, though."

Rachel's eyes brightened, the penny dropping at last. The thought that had been staring her in the face up until now revealed itself.

"One of the bucket list tour is the ringleader," she announced.

"Right again."

"How did you work it out? I've only just arrived at the conclusion myself. That's why they're on the same deck!"

"It's obvious there has to be a link between the bucket list group and the couple your ex has been following. They have been seen speaking to members of that party on numerous occasions. Although it narrows down the field to forty-three, it doesn't solve the case, but it does give us the opportunity to look into every one of them. I've got the security team working on that now."

"Did Robert's boss manage to give you any leads?"

"No, just what we already know. He was understandably more concerned about one of his team being in an Australian prison and one being a mole. He had already been informed about Mrs Chowdry. We left it that he would look into all of their backgrounds and let us know if he came up with anything."

"So there is a murderer in that group. I can't help thinking now that Mrs F's death must have something to do with this case. It would be too much of a coincidence for it not to."

"My thoughts entirely. She could have been one of the ringleaders, for all we know," said Waverley.

"What makes you think it's not the son or his wife?"

"The purser has confirmed they were both with him at the time of her murder."

"I'm surprised Chief Heel didn't look into the bucket list tour party," Sarah interjected. Rachel had been thinking the same thing.

"Well, erm, as you know, Heel is not a well man. He was also convinced that there was enough evidence against Mr Janda initially to warrant his arrest. Having considered the evidence myself, I concluded he was quite right in his assumption. It was only after he found out the snake wasn't venomous that it seemed less likely.

"It still doesn't clear Janda because a snake container was found in his room, and it was an Indian snake used as subterfuge in the attack. He has no alibi and he has knowledge of anaesthesia that could have served to help him smuggle the snake on board. To scanners, it would not be picked up if it didn't move. He is also the most likely person to have access to the sort of poison used to kill Mrs Flanders, topped off with the fact he knew the woman before, had been in communication with her, and she trusted him enough to take a drink if he offered her one. He remains at the top of the suspect list for that crime, as far as I am concerned."

"So the poisonous nerve agent was in the drink then?"

"Yes, it was analysed in Melbourne and traces of the poison hemlock were isolated."

"How awful, but I still don't believe Deep did it. She was the love of his life, the one that got away, and he was excited about meeting up with her again. There's no way he would have done that in order to kill her, and I'm absolutely certain he has nothing to do with the other racket."

"Unfortunately, the butler didn't see who Mrs Flanders drank with as he was attending to guests in the other suite at the time. I don't like to think it, Rachel, but we can't rule out the possibility of two killers," answered Waverley.

"No, the MO of our killer makes me think it's the same person. Both the murder and the attempted murder involved framing a person close to the victim to draw attention away from the real perpetrator. I think that person is exceptionally devious and clever, and deadly. It also makes the attack on Sunita Chowdry premeditated."

Waverley took a few notes as Rachel spoke, then lifted his head, brushing his hand through his thin greying hair.

"You might be right, it could well be someone other than Janda, but Rachel, please don't dice with death this time. The killer could be on to you, and I can't protect you if you don't tell me what you're up to. Last night was a near miss – it could have been the killer in your room. Let me handle it."

"He's right, Rachel. You could have been killed last night, and this involves more than one bad guy, a mole, a ringleader – or two – not to mention that Scheffler couple."

What they said made sense, but Rachel was unconvinced Waverley was going after the right people. If he wasted precious time looking into Deep, the real killer was likely to get away with it. She was almost certain she had met the killer of Mrs F, and if this person was also responsible for the attack on Sunita Chowdry and the framing of Robert, it was highly likely they knew of her links to him. She might not be able to stay out of it even if she wanted to, and one thing was certain: she would rather be the hunter than the prey.

"Rachel?" Waverley was frowning again.

"Please, Rachel." Sarah's pleading eyes bored into her own. She was being backed into a corner and she didn't want to lie to her best friend.

"Okay, I agree to do my best to stay out of the matter, but if someone comes after me, I have to be prepared, so I will put in place a contingency plan for my own protection."

"That's not exactly what I wanted to hear," said Waverley.

"It's the best I can offer you, take it or leave it."

The security chief took in a deep breath and exhaled slowly. "I'll take it. Promise me that if you stumble across anything, you will come to me first."

"I promise."

Waverley stood and walked them to the door.

"I mean it, Rachel. Me first."

She nodded.

Chapter 27

Rachel and Sarah remained quiet after the meeting with Waverley, each woman lost in her own thoughts. Rachel put her arm through her friend's to let her know she was still there.

"Don't worry, Sarah. At least we've narrowed the field and Chowdry and the Schefflers will be watched closely by Waverley's team."

"I know, I just can't help remembering that poor woman lying behind a rock. Whoever did that to her is ruthless and calculated. It was only by chance we happened to stumble across her, although I fear we might have been too late. I worry whether I could have done anything else to save her. What if I missed something?"

Rachel realised Sarah was going through the all-too-familiar thought processes experienced by anyone working in the emergency services. For the police it was "What if I'd got there a few minutes earlier? What if I missed a vital clue?" For Sarah, and she supposed for doctors and paramedics too, it was the fear of not doing enough to save a life or forgetting to do something vitally important that could make the difference between life and death.

"Sarah, you did everything you could under the circumstances. You cleared her airway, stemmed the bleeding and moved her into the recovery position, giving her the best chance. You're not a brain surgeon, and even if you were, you couldn't have done any more out there in the countryside. The woman is alive because of what you did."

"Thanks, Rachel. I've been through it with Graham and he agrees with you, so I guess I know it really, it's just so horrible. This killer is evil, though. First he kills Mrs F in such a way as to ensure she suffers terribly before dying, and then he hits Sunita with a rock and leaves her to die slowly out there in the open while planting evidence to incriminate scumbag."

They both laughed as Sarah lightened up with her favourite reference to Robert.

"You're right, this person is evil, but Waverley will catch him or her."

"You don't think a woman could have done this, do you?"

"I've learned it's better not to be sexist when it comes to evil. Although the majority of killers are men, this sort of thing doesn't fit with the work of the majority of killers. If it is the same killer, an elderly lady and a beautiful young woman have been attacked, so there's no pattern other than the killer had enough knowledge to try to pin the murder and attempted murder on to another person. If we didn't know about Robert's investigation and the link between the Schefflers and the bucket list cruisers, we would be spitting in the wind."

"Ugh! Is that a police expression? It doesn't sound right coming out of your mouth."

Rachel felt suitably chastised. "Mm, I don't think Marjorie would approve either. Come on, let's go to Creams for tea."

Once they were seated, Rachel ordered a cinnamon roll and Sarah opted for lemon meringue pie. They also requested a pot of coffee. The waiter was the same one who had taken a shine to Sarah in the past, but who had never plucked up courage to ask her out, and now Jason was well and truly on the scene.

After the waiter had delivered coffee and desserts, pouring the coffee for them, Rachel looked at her friend.

"Have you spoken to Jason yet?"

"No, I haven't had the chance. I was on call last night, as you know. I thought he might be at the meeting today. At least we got off lightly with the incursion into scumbag's room."

Rachel took a sip of coffee and bit off a chunk of cinnamon roll. "I expect Waverley's got him looking into the bucket list passengers as well as the Flanders and the Schefflers. No matter what he says, he'll want to rule out Joe or Chloe Flanders from paying someone to do away with his mother."

"Poor Jason, I'm sure you're right. He'll be pulling in double shifts to get to the bottom of this."

"He'll need to before anyone else gets hurt."

"Oh you don't think that will happen, do you?"

"I don't know. The annoying thing is I can't work out a motive for both attacks. The attack on Sunita is almost certainly to do with Robert's investigation, but the attack on Mrs Flanders? That seems more personal." Rachel took another slurp of coffee and rubbed her temple before looking up at Sarah. "Unless the Flanders business is tied up with the smuggling racket and she was either involved or got wind of it, resulting in her demise. Charles did say the Schefflers were interested in buying the travel agency."

"But what about the threatening letters she told Deep about?"

Rachel scrunched up her face. "Might have been a ruse to throw us off the scent."

"There's no 'us' anymore, Rachel. You heard Waverley, this killer – or killers – is dangerous and they could be on to you. I'm surprised he's not put you under protective guard."

"Whatever you do, don't put that idea into his head. I wouldn't put it past him to do it."

"How did your class go this morning?"

"It went well except Glenis was a bit off with me, while the usually caustic Emma was positively ebullient. For her, anyway."

"People can be strange. What have you done to upset Glenis?"

"No idea, unless missing dinner with the bucket listers last night after her generously inviting me on their day trip constituted a moral crime."

"Come to think of it, she did seem a bit miffed when we met her on Robert's deck, didn't she?"

"Oh, you've remembered he has a name then! Yes, that's the only thing that would explain it. I'll make sure I meet them for dinner tonight and see if I can get back on good terms. I forgot to tell you, speaking of people wandering around on different decks, I found a very confused Patty being chased down my corridor by Emma last night."

The comical image of the stick insect chasing the voluptuous and muddled Patty down the corridor sent the young women into shrieks of laughter.

"As much as I dislike Emma – this morning's behaviour aside, that is – she does have the unenviable task of keeping her confused charge under control."

"A job for which she is very well remunerated, from what we understand."

Rachel almost leapt out of her skin as a bony hand touched her shoulder.

"What the—"

"I'm sorry. Did I startle you?" Stick insect Emma didn't look sorry at all. Rachel wondered how much of the conversation she had overheard.

"Emma, how nice to see you. Is everything alright?" Sarah intervened.

Alcohol breath almost knocked Rachel out as the woman answered. "I seem to have lost Patty again. I was wondering if you had seen her recently."

Rachel's head moved backwards automatically as the other woman leaned in closer. "Erm, no, sorry. I haven't. Perhaps one of your friends has found her?"

"Mm, maybe." Emma leaned in closer still and Rachel was running out of neck to stretch her head back any further. "They seem to be more your friends than mine," she hissed.

Rachel stared into the flashing glazed grey eyes of the woman towering over her, who remained there for an uncomfortably long time before standing upright again.

"Right, well, I'll go and look elsewhere then."

Rachel and Sarah stared after the woman, who somehow managed to walk in a straight line on exiting the patisserie.

"What on earth was that all about?" Sarah's eyebrows formed an upside-down V-shape as her eyes remained fixed on the exit.

"Your guess is as good as mine. I take everything back about her being friendlier after that little encounter. The woman's clearly as unhinged as her friend, although it could be the alcohol. Did you get the stench?"

"It did manage to waft its way over, yes. I'm sorry, I didn't see her coming or I would have warned you. Do you think she overheard our conversation?"

"I doubt it, she was like a bull in a china shop. I can't imagine she paused before scaring me half to death. I can still feel the cold chill over my shoulder blade, and her eyes – anger personified. I feel like I need a shower. I pity Patty when she tracks her down."

"Pity Patty, I like that one." Sarah giggled and they returned to the remainder of their coffee.

After Sarah left to shower and change uniform for evening surgery, Rachel took a stroll around the upper decks. It was a balmy spring day with temperatures remaining a pleasant twenty degrees. The sun glowed on to the swimming pool where passengers were enjoying late afternoon swims while a live band played pop music from the eighties.

Rachel leaned against a rail and felt relaxed again as the surroundings calmed her, despite the rising waves breaking against the ship's passage. A storm had been forecast for this evening, the captain had announced during his broadcast that resonated all around the ship every morning and evening like clockwork.

As Rachel stood gazing down on the Tasman Sea, it made her realise how small the gigantic *Coral Queen* was when compared with nature. At times like these, she was pleased she believed in God. She looked up to the heavens and uttered a silent prayer, remembering who it was that she believed was in overall charge of her world.

The dark clouds in the faraway distance were moving closer as she returned to the stateroom to wash and change for dinner. She debated ordering room service, but thought it would be best to try and patch things up with Glenis, even if she wasn't sure what it was that needed patching up. Perhaps the sparrow-like woman liked to have more control than Rachel had given her credit for. Whatever it was, Glenis had been kind and accommodating to her, so she would do her best to remain on good terms. Rachel was not a moody person herself, but that didn't mean she couldn't understand that some people had a tendency to mood swings.

It must be exhausting.

Rachel sighed. *There's enough going on in the world as it is without having to deal with unpredictable moods.*

She smiled as she dressed for the evening, thankful that although she and Sarah were different in so many ways, neither of them bore grudges or went into sulks. The two women often used to joke that they only remained friends because they had different tastes in men, and their friendship had indeed withstood the test of time. Although there were occasions during adolescence when, battered by hormones, they would have arguments, they always managed to patch it up.

Chapter 28

The main restaurant, aptly named the Coral Restaurant, was as busy as ever. The maître d', dressed in his immaculately tailored cream suit, stood out from the other waiters who wore black suits and white bow ties. He quickly and efficiently assigned tables or marked off guests arriving to eat, and then directed waiters to escort them.

While waiting in the queue, Rachel took the time to admire the huge expanse of the two-tiered restaurant that stretched from midships and filled the rear part of deck four. Chandeliers hung down from the ceiling, providing glittering illumination over the whole restaurant. At various points, etched marble pillars stood tall, adding to the lavish effect.

To the right and left, or starboard and port side as Sarah called them, were crystal-clear rectangular windows with rounded edges. This was the place where people who wanted to dress up for the evening ate before or after taking in a show or availing themselves of any of the other multitudinous activities offered on board ship.

Rachel now thought of the *Coral Queen* as a village with a population of around five-and-a-half thousand people. The main village population was the crew. Then there were the villagers, who spent as much time as possible on the ship: these were repeat cruisers, some of whom almost lived aboard! Finally there were the visitors, passengers numbering around three-and-a-half thousand who were sailing either for the first time or less frequently than the regulars. This way of studying the ship made her feel more at home. Cruising to her was becoming like visiting family, except that each time she visited, the bonus was that she discovered new places and met new people.

In spite of the puzzling murder of Mrs Flanders, the attack on Sunita Chowdry and concern about Robert being in an Australian prison, she felt she was experiencing the cruise of a lifetime. Australia had lived up to its reputation and the weather was divine, except for this evening. The ship was starting to roll and list as the anticipated storm drew in.

It won't be long before many passengers will call it a night and lie down before they fall down. Rachel chuckled inwardly.

"Miss Prince, a pleasure to see you this evening. Are you enjoying your cruise?" The maître d' was the same Colin Bell she had met on several cruises.

"Hello, Colin. Immensely, thank you."

"Will you be eating at your table this evening or with our special guests?" His eyes twinkled and the laughter lines around them revealed his love of people.

"With your special guests, please."

"In that case—" With an arm gesture that wouldn't look out of place among royalty, he invited her to follow an eagerly awaiting waiter. "Table 507," he informed the waiter, smiling at Rachel and then diverting his attention to the next guests in line.

The restaurant was packed and filled with laughter as guests enjoyed their five-course dining experience. Rachel was pleased to see the usual vacant space beside Deep and wondered for the first time why it was always there before head-slapping herself inwardly.

Of course! The space had been reserved for Mrs Flanders. How hard it must be for Deep to sit there each night. She was surprised the place hadn't been taken away, but the awful reality hit Rachel that it was kept in place for her. The realisation made her feel sick to the stomach that she might be adding to his pain, yet humbled that the group welcomed her so much, there was always a place for her.

Glenis's eyes lit up when she saw Rachel and she immediately left off speaking to Emma, drawing daggers from the sticklike woman and a grimace from Rachel. Nevertheless, she was pleased Glenis appeared to have got over whatever it was she had been annoyed about.

"Rachel, you're joining us this evening. That's wonderful."

Heads turned in her direction as the men stood and waited for her to be seated, an old habit that this wonderful group still adhered to. The waiter pulled out a chair for her and she had to stifle a giggle as the men sat down in unison.

Grow up, Prince, she chastised herself.

"I'm sorry I missed it last night, but I was with my friend, Sarah. She'd had a long day working, so we ate together." Rachel neglected to mention her passing out and ending up in the infirmary.

Deep's gaze was penetrating as usual and the raised side of one brow told her he knew she was being economical with the truth. He really did remind her of her father who could see right through her, but always allowed her to tell him everything when she was ready to.

"Pleased you could join us this evening," Deep said. "The place next to me seems empty without you." His wistful eyes confirmed what Rachel had suspected. Of course, Mrs F would have been the one to draw up a plan of table places for the tour group.

A glimmer of recognition that this was significant nestled itself into Rachel's brain. Was this Mrs F's main suspect list all seated around the same table? If so, was the woman on the right track? Something she would explore later.

"How was your day?" she asked Deep. Glenis was now occupied with Prudence, and Emma was filling her wine glass, a faux pas in this group where the men preferred to pour drinks for the ladies. Rachel had picked this up on the first evening. It was a different world to the one she had grown up in and she liked it. Some feminists might baulk at the behaviour, and Rachel, an independent-minded woman, had mixed feelings about it, but it didn't appear to have held these women back. Many of them were accomplished in what they did and had held down highly successful business positions. Others, though, may have been overly dependent on their spouses or partners and lacked opportunities to be viewed equally.

"You seem deep in thought, Rachel," remarked Prudence as the waiter stood behind her right shoulder, waiting for her to order hors d'oeuvres.

"Oh sorry, I was miles away, looking at the purple sky out there." Rachel noticed – just in time – the stormy but beautiful purple sky through one of the windows.

"Australian skies can be magnificent, ma'am," said the waiter, "but the skies over Africa take some beating." The South African accent suggested he might be slightly biased, but what did she know? "Hors d'oeuvre, madam?"

Rachel ordered anchovies followed by Caesar salad, and for the main she requested sea bass with cauliflower and wild mushrooms.

Patty appeared as confused as ever, staring around the table as if she didn't know what was going on and repeatedly asking why she was here and where they were.

"We're having dinner, Patty. On holiday, remember?"

Patty clearly didn't remember. "Holiday? Oh, I see." The befuddled woman looked as if she thought it might be a trap. "If you say so, but who are these people? They're not all English." A glare was fired towards Deep, suggesting she might be racist. Deep smiled at her sympathetically.

"No, dear," Glenis interjected. "I'm Welsh for a start." This brought a chuckle from those around who had been listening in to the conversation.

"Sorry," said Patty, her eyes still darting around anxiously.

"You're on a ship off the coast of Australia, Patty. We all are, we're on our way to New Zealand, but tomorrow we have another sea day." Glenis's voice went up quite a few decibels, as if she thought that by raising it, she could make the confused woman understand better.

"That's nice. I like the sea, don't I, Emma?"

"Do you? Yes, of course you do." Emma had taken the opportunity to help herself to another refill while everyone's attention was focussed on Patty.

When the conversations moved on to other matters and Patty's attention was diverted by Emma, Glenis leaned across the table.

"She's been quite with it today, and now this. Poor thing, she does seem to go in and out of reality."

Rachel nodded; there was nothing she could think of to say. Her experience of dementia sufferers was thankfully limited, skewed towards those with violent paranoia who were often brought to the attention of the police.

"You've gone again, Rachel." This time it was Deep who drew her from her musings.

"Oh dear, I'm sorry. I was just thinking about an experience at work."

"You haven't told us what you do, Rachel." Glenis's interest was piqued.

"And neither should she," answered Deep on Rachel's behalf. "Otherwise all us old biddies would grill the girl *ad nauseum*. She's on holiday, let her keep some of her life secrets. She has just been showing me her engagement ring."

That worked. Rachel mouthed "Thank you" to Deep as the others cooed over her ring all over again and wanted to know all about the love of her life, so Rachel brought up a photo of Carlos on her mobile phone.

"Oh my word! Now he is handsome, I'm almost jealous," said Prudence with a flirtatious look towards Charles.

In between firing darts at Rachel with her eyes, Emma took every opportunity for surreptitious refills and became more venomous with every additional drink.

Nobody took any notice, so she had yet another drink, eyeing Rachel with hostility.

After dinner, Rachel excused herself, but promised to join the bucket listers in the Stars Ballroom tomorrow for the next round of the singing competition. It had now been whittled down to twelve, with Prudence still in the running.

Deep's moroseness concerned Rachel. He was clearly suffering and longing to go home and forget about the whole Florence Flanders episode, but he had been forbidden to leave the ship for now. But the idea that had come to her over dinner gave Rachel hope that she would be able to solve the case soon.

Straightening up her shoulders, she headed back to her room to carry out some research.

Chapter 29

Before handing over the laptop and files belonging to Florence Flanders to Jason, Rachel had photographed the contents of what she considered to be important. Now she opened up her laptop where the files had been automatically transferred from her iPhone; it was time to study them in more detail and see if she could piece together the bits of information she already had.

Her research was short lived as the ship listed and rolled in the storm that was now very much present. The captain had informed them they were in for a rough eight hours and to take care in public places. As Rachel tried to stand, she was thrown back on to the bed. She succeeded on the second attempt and walked unsteadily towards the balcony windows.

The night sky was a dark purple when lit up by streaks of lightning, which flashed every few minutes. Sheets of rain traversed her view and loud claps of thunder could be heard above music from lounges. The rolling of the ship was worse than she had ever experienced since she'd started cruising, and even the giant *Coral Queen* felt like a small fish in a very large pond.

The huge, undulating waves were mesmerising to watch, although Rachel didn't dare open the balcony doors as the captain had warned everyone to stick to indoor areas. The balcony chairs and table were fastened down. Feeling like a small child learning to walk, she made her way back to the bed and tried to continue with her research.

The phone rang.

"Hello, Rachel. Just checking you're alright."

"I'm fine, Sarah, but how bad is it going to get?"

A sudden surge threw her laptop across the bed and she clung on to it before it fell.

"Not too much worse than this. The captain's racing ahead of the storm; he's raised the stabilisers which is why we're feeling it more. We're in for a few hours of really rough seas before the worst of the storm crosses behind us. All the medical team are on duty as passengers are calling left, right and centre."

"Poor you, it's going to be a busy night then. I'm glad I don't usually get sick, although I'm not promising."

"Well if you do, I hope you've brought your own Stugeron as the shop's sold out and we've only got injectables left! Most passengers come prepared, though. Unfortunately the combination of booze, sickness and motion is creating problems with falls. We've already had two fractures to deal with."

"Don't worry about me, Sarah. I'll be fine; you be careful too, though."

"I will, and thankfully I don't get seasick either, but Brigitte does. Gwen's given her a pack of her own seasick pills to tide her over the next few hours. Speak to you in the morning."

"Okay, bye."

Another flash of lightning filled the night sky. Darkness had fallen during dinner like a curtain closing, as if the clear skies above wanted to be away from the storm. Rachel wasn't frightened; she knew the ship would outrun the storm and the *Coral* could cope with most of the elements, as long as there wasn't a tsunami.

In order to shake that last thought from her head, she opened the laptop for the third time. This time she felt she was getting somewhere. Mrs Flanders had left some very deliberate clues as to who she imagined was behind the poisonous emails. The question marks, Rachel had worked out, did indicate her list of suspects; Mrs F had even put a question mark next to Deep's name at one stage, but then crossed it out again.

Another lurch of the ship and the constant rolling was making Rachel feel queasy, so she decided to call it a night and get ready for bed.

As the ship rocked and rolled throughout the night, so did Rachel's thoughts. She had a nagging feeling that once again she was missing something important.

Noise from the corridor outside and a television playing full blast woke her up the next morning. She groaned and pulled the pillow over her head, but was unable to get back to sleep.

The ship was moving smoothly once again as if the storm had been a distant dream. At least it had been a night storm; it would have been much more dangerous for passengers and crew during the daytime when people wanted to continue as if nothing was happening and crew had to battle the elements to keep them happy.

Rachel opted to go straight for breakfast as she had another class to teach today, and she suspected it might be an interesting and revealing one. Maybe it was just wishful thinking, but she was feeling optimistic.

The buffet was packed with tired looking passengers, some still drugged from anti-sickness remedies and others from lack of sleep. The waiters' cheery voices, greetings and singing soon brought the majority back into holiday mode. Rachel hadn't heard from Sarah since she woke up and assumed her friend was trying to catch a few hours' sleep before morning surgery.

"I thought I'd find you here." Chowdry placed his tray opposite her without asking if she was happy for him to join her. He looked edgy.

"What are you doing here? If you're being watched, I don't want people to think I'm involved in your investigation." The earlier sympathy she had felt towards him had changed to bristly contempt after hearing he had also been in Robert's room.

"The case is being shut down anyway. We don't have enough evidence and the people we've been watching haven't put a foot out of line."

I'm not surprised with such an incompetent and dysfunctional group on their tail. Rachel kept those thoughts to herself.

"Nevertheless, I still don't want to be identified with any of you, thank you."

"Did anyone ever tell you, you need to relax more?" He leered across the table and Rachel resisted the temptation to throw her coffee over him.

"How is your wife?" She almost spat the words out as she stared hard back at him.

He looked away for a moment. "Still in a coma, the doctors are not sure if she'll come out of it." At least there was a hint of regret in his voice. "But it's over as far as I'm concerned. She had an affair, remember? With *your* ex. I would say it's high time we got back at both of them. How about it?"

Now Rachel saw where he was going to with this. He had some sick notion that if he got off with her, he would be getting his own back on Robert.

"I don't know how men like you live with all that raging testosterone and one-upmanship going on inside you. This is not a game; your wife has been severely injured and all you want to do is play tit for tat! I wouldn't go out with a man like you if you were the last remaining man on earth. I do hope I've made myself clear."

Rachel pushed back her chair and left him glaring after her.

As she marched through the corridor towards the stairs, she bumped into Patty.

"Oh, I'm so sorry. Are you okay?" The woman was actually built of stern stuff and Rachel had literally bounced off her, but felt it polite to ask.

"You should watch where you're going. Do I know you?"

"We've met a few times at dinner and you come to my self-defence class."

Patty's eyes narrowed before the glazed look took over. "What am I doing here?" she asked.

"I expect you are going for breakfast. Look, here's Glenis and Prudence, I'm sure they'll help you." Rachel looked pleadingly towards the two women as they exited the lifts.

"Of course we will," said Glenis. "Come along with us, Patty. No Emma today?"

"No I don't think so," answered the confused older woman.

"I expect she's got a headache." Prudence winked at Rachel.

"Yes, she did knock it back a bit last night – probably the only one on board who got any sleep," said Glenis. "That was some storm, wasn't it?"

The women took their charge towards the buffet, relieving Rachel so she could return to her room before class.

The self-defence class was only half full and most of the attendees seemed tired, so Rachel got them up doing some one-on-one moves to help wake them. She was itching to get the class over with as she needed to get back to her stateroom and check out the data on her laptop. She now felt certain the answer was in there somewhere and was determined to find it.

This morning she had felt frustrated. She hated the fact the case was going nowhere, and now the police investigation into the Schefflers had also been brought to a standstill. They might never find out who the ringleader of the smuggling business was or who attacked Sunita Chowdry. What was worse, Robert might be left rotting in an Australian jail for a crime he didn't commit. While she had come to terms with having no romantic feelings towards him, she did believe his account of the day she and Sarah had stumbled across Sunita.

With only five days left of the cruise to go, she had to get to the bottom of this conundrum, or a person or persons unknown would be getting away with murder. She had narrowed the list of suspects down, but was no nearer to knowing who the culprit was. Perhaps it was time for her and Waverley to share information, but she didn't really have any concrete leads and he'd made it clear on previous cruises he wasn't interested in hunches. This was still in the hunch stage, and without more to go on Waverley would just be annoyed with her for continuing to investigate when he'd told her not to.

After ordering a room service lunch, Rachel opened up the laptop and once again stared at the information in front of her. The question marks next to names amounted to eighteen in total, the circled ones telling Rachel Mrs F felt she had narrowed the list of most likely suspects down to six. Her head pounded with frustration as she went through every item she had photographed, certain she was missing the obvious.

After looking through the documents and photos, she poured a glass of water and stared out at the crystal-clear blue sky. All was calm outside, but there was increasing turmoil in her head. It was time to do a replay of the events since boarding.

"I'm over thinking this, I know I am. The answer lies in the simple things."

Finally a memory popped into her head and she believed that held the answer to one of the mysteries, but there was no evidence. She opened the laptop from its sleep mode and stared again at a photo that she had passed over each time she'd looked at it.

Jumping up from the chair and racing down to the Coral Supermarket, she found what she was looking for and took it to the till. Once she was back in her room, she pulled the magnifying glass out of the paper bag it had been wrapped in and used it to scan the photo that she was sure held the answer to this mystery.

It had been there, staring at her all along. She didn't know if this was the ringleader of the smuggling racket for certain, but she knew who had killed Mrs F.

The telephone rang. Rachel felt breathless with excitement as she answered.

Chapter 30

The infirmary had been heaving all night with people needing treatment for storm-induced hyperemesis. There had also been a fair share of cuts and bruises, and two broken bones. On top of that, the medical team had been all over the ship, treating passengers in their rooms or reassuring them that the *Coral Queen* was not going to sink.

One woman had had such a bad panic attack, Graham had needed to sedate her with intramuscular midazolam. Sarah had checked on her this morning and her husband reported that she had slept all night and was fine now. He apologised for any inconvenience they had caused and Sarah reassured him that his wife was not the only one who had been frightened, subtly neglecting to report that she had been the worst.

The team were being served coffee in Gwen's office. Bleary-eyed, they relaxed back and were all pleased the night was over.

"That was one of the worst nights in a long time." Graham voiced what they each felt.

"I don't want to see any more puke," said Bernard.

"And I don't want to be reminded of it, thank you." Gwen shot Bernard a withering stare.

"Sorry. How are you, Brigitte?"

Brigitte looked pale; she had suffered in the early part of the storm, until Gwen's tablets had helped make her feel better.

"I don't feel too good," she replied.

"Why don't you go to bed, Brigitte?" said Gwen. "We'll cover the surgery and I'll take your morning's on call. You can relieve me after lunch."

"Thank you," said Brigitte, wasting no time before heading towards the door. Sarah was worried she might be sick again.

"I think I'm going to go and have a hearty breakfast with the family," said Graham. "Thank you for helping out with them last night, Gwen. They didn't enjoy the storm at all."

"You're welcome. I don't know how you can talk about food, though. I don't think I'll ever eat again."

"Ah, you'll be back to normal later. It's all in the mind."

"Tell Brigitte that," said Sarah. "Where's Alex?"

"Gone for a lie down – he was a bit queasy as well," said Gwen.

"I'm going to write up all my visits from last night, I've got pockets full of paper," said Sarah.

She wanted to check something else that had been nagging her at the back of her mind, but she hadn't had any time, having been up most of the night and manning the infirmary since 5am. Graham had discharged the passengers when he came in at eight before the team retired for coffee.

Powering up the computer in one of the treatment rooms, Sarah went straight to the records she was looking for. It took a few strokes of the keyboard before the answer to what had been niggling her jumped out on the screen.

She picked up the phone immediately and dialled Rachel's number. Her friend answered, sounding excited.

"Rachel, I know who killed Mrs F and why."

"I've just worked it out myself. How did you find out?"

"I was called to quite a few emergencies on deck seven last night and something odd popped up, but I haven't had time until just now to follow it through. The answer is in the medical records and it's been there all along."

"That does sound interesting. I think we've got enough to prove who killed Mrs Flanders, but I still need to piece together a few more bits about the other crime. Shall we meet up in Waverley's office? Could you also call Jason and ask him a question as I think it might hold the key to the attack on Sunita Chowdry?" Rachel relayed the query.

"Will do. I'll see you in half an hour."

Chapter 31

Waverley listened while Rachel and Sarah recounted the evidence they had come across and why it was significant. He stroked his chin thoughtfully, but didn't interrupt except to ask a few questions for clarification. He tapped his rapidly becoming portly abdomen and looked satisfied before instructing the two officers present, Jason and Ravanos.

"Bring them all here."

Rachel and Sarah enjoyed a cup of coffee while they waited anxiously, knowing that if they weren't careful, the slippery killer could still get away.

Jason arrived first accompanied by Deep Janda and Jack Chowdry. Next came Ravanos with the two women. All four appeared confused and didn't know where to look.

"What's the meaning of this, Chief?" asked Chowdry, clearly deciding it was time to break the silence.

"I'll come to that in a minute," replied Waverley, enjoying the moment. "Mr Janda, please could you take a look at this photograph and think carefully before answering. Do you recognise the woman to the right of the picture?" Waverley handed copies of the photo to the other guests in the room.

Deep took the photo from Waverley's hand and donned a pair of reading glasses. At first his eyes focussed on the happy embrace of the young couple who sixty years ago had been deeply in love. He forced his eyes away to stare at the woman on the right. His eyes scrunched and he shook his head.

"No, I'm sorry, I don't know who that is."

A gasp came from one of the elderly women present and a glare that could turn a man to stone, both of which were missed by Deep as he looked again at the ancient photo of himself with Florence Flanders.

"Please sit down, Mr Janda, and the rest of you."

The group obeyed and took all the available seating in Waverley's office. Rachel crouched down next to Deep and patted him comfortingly on the arm.

Chowdry was becoming impatient. "We have a right to know what we are doing here," he yelled.

"Ah, Mr Chowdry, I understand that on the day of your wife's attack, you were with Mrs Chambers here?" All eyes turned towards Patty as the bemused woman looked on. Stick insect just sat and glared at Rachel.

"I was. I've already been over this before, so if that's all, I'm leaving."

Jason put a firm hand on Chowdry's shoulder, keeping him in the chair.

"Do you remember being with this man, Mrs Chambers?"

"Yes," answered Patty.

Convenient, thought Rachel, but said nothing.

"Can I go now?" asked Chowdry.

"No-one leaves this room until I'm finished." Waverley raised his voice, bringing an instant silence into the room. "Chowdry, I'm going to ask you again, and this time I want the truth. But before I do so, I'm going to warn you that the person you asked to give you the alibi to cover for your clandestine meeting with the Schefflers needed the alibi more than you did."

"What do you mean?" Chowdry looked straight over to Patty as realisation dawned. "You attacked Sunita." Tears filled his eyes.

"I don't know what you're talking about. What's happening, Emma?"

"You can cut the pretence." Rachel glared at the woman. "You're no more demented than I am, but it was a nice act. You are the leader of an international smuggling and money laundering ring. That fact fell in to place when I remembered your so-called accidental bumping into Harrison Scheffler the other day when you most likely exchanged information of some sort. You probably don't usually do the dirty work yourself, but on this occasion you had a personal vendetta. One that's eaten away at you for six decades. You wanted to get back at the woman you believed took away the man you loved. Truth is, she didn't. Both of them left that relationship broken hearted, but you hunted her down like an animal and finally got your revenge."

"You're talking nonsense," Emma snapped. "Patty is not a well woman and I'd thank you to leave her alone."

Rachel ignored the outburst and continued. "The photo in your hand is one of you, funnily enough with the same look of hatred in your eyes as you have now. There you are staring on at your imaginary lover – the man who didn't even know you existed, so couldn't possibly remember who you were."

"He loves me. He always has, you have no idea. How dare you speak to me like this!" Patty pushed away the hand of Emma, who was trying to get her to be quiet. Rachel had been banking on this response and now she had it. "He's mine."

"What is this woman talking about?" asked Deep. "Did she kill Florence?"

"Of course I killed your whore! She took you away from me." Wild eyes flashed dangerously towards Deep. "I'm the one you love, don't you realise?"

Deep stood and stared sorrowfully at Patty. "Woman, I don't know you, and you've done a terrible thing." He looked towards Waverley, who nodded and let him leave the room with his dignity still intact.

Patty burst into tears.

Waverley continued above her moans. "Madam, I am arresting you for the murder of Florence Flanders and for the attempted murder of Sunita Chowdry. You will be handed over to the port authorities in the morning where you will most likely be deported back to Australia to face charges there. I'm certain we will also find further evidence of your links to the smuggling ring Miss Prince has alluded to when we go through your room."

"How did you find out the rest?" a perfectly lucid Patty stopped crying as if she'd flicked a switch and turned to Rachel.

"It took some time because you were quite clever. A number of people remarked on how sane you were one minute, and then how bemused you could be the next. Dr Bentley has confirmed that this can sometimes happen, but you gave yourself away a number of times when hatred spilled out of your eyes towards Deep. At first, I thought I was imagining things, but the longer the cruise went on, the more your act lapsed.

"Your name was one of six circled on a list kept by Florence Flanders, who I believe had almost narrowed it down to you. She made the fatal mistake of letting you into her room on boarding day. I expect you fooled her with the confused act that you've used throughout the cruise. She offered you a drink, and most likely while her back was turned, you added hemlock to her drink and cynically watched her gulp it back before she went to meet with Deep in the library. You followed her, or maybe got there first with the snake in your handbag, and as the poison took effect, you gloated over your evil plan and brought out the snake to bite her on the heel. Seeing Deep heading towards the library, you stabbed her in the chest – with a knife you probably had with you in case she didn't fall for the drink plan – to draw attention away from the snake bite.

"I suspect your original plan was for her to be found dead from an unidentified snakebite. Unfortunately for you, Deep arrived and you couldn't retrieve the snake in time, so you managed to plant a snake box in his room while everyone else was busy attending to the dead woman. But there's one thing I don't understand – why would you frame the man you say you love?"

"Unrequited love?" suggested Waverley. Patty glared at them both.

Rachel continued, "My friend here also discovered you had listed Manandeep Janda as your next of kin. Deluded to the end."

"That woman got what she deserved, and so will you because I will hunt you down sometime in the future and make sure you join her."

"I very much doubt that. You will spend the rest of your miserable life behind bars." Rachel held Patty's gaze.

"Why did you attack Sunita?" asked Chowdry, looking stricken. "I thought we had a deal?"

"I noticed your boss making a play for our Miss Prim here and overheard the conversation she had at the dinner table that night. You told us your boss was on to us and I saw him flirting with your wife. It was obvious how to get rid of him."

"You tried to frame him for murder, but the young woman lived," Waverley intervened.

"Barely," Patty snorted and cackled loudly. "Nobody makes a fool out of me."

"Take this woman to the brig," Waverley ordered.

"Can I go now?" asked Chowdry.

"I'm afraid not. You are the mole that has been working against your own team and you gave that murderous woman an alibi. You will be placed under house arrest until the port authorities decide how to deal with you."

Chowdry dropped his head. "I had no idea she would stoop to this and I didn't know anything about the other woman she's apparently killed."

"You're a criminal, Mr Chowdry, I don't have any sympathy for you. Take him away, Goodridge."

"Yes, sir." Jason left the room with Chowdry.

"You're very quiet, Emma," said Rachel, glaring at the stick insect who sat stiffened in the chair.

"I had no idea."

"I think you did," said Waverley. "You are on the payroll. You may not have wanted to be involved in murder – we will never know that – but you covered for her, helping with her pretence of suffering from early dementia. You will also be held under house arrest and handed over to the port authorities."

"I knew you were trouble the moment I laid eyes on you," Emma snarled at Rachel.

"Likewise," answered Rachel, allowing herself a moment's smugness.

Chapter 32

Later that evening, Rachel and Sarah joined Glenis and the others in the Stars Ballroom to watch the finals of the singing competition. Rachel sat next to Deep, who appeared relaxed.

"How are you?" she asked gently.

"Relieved that my name has been cleared and the person responsible for Florence's death has been caught, thanks to you."

"I'm relieved too." Rachel took a sip of Martini.

"I didn't know that woman. How did she become so cruel?"

"Who knows? She became obsessed with you, and felt spurned, in her warped mind you had always been her lover. Don't feel sorry for her, though. What she did was evil. A cold-blooded killer, she was determined to mete out revenge on the woman she held responsible for her misery."

"How did she track her down?"

"It was most probably quite by chance. On booking a place for her and Emma on the bucket list tour in order to meet up with the Schefflers, she must have discovered that the travel agency was owned by the person who in her mind was her archenemy. The poison emails can be linked to the day of her booking the cruise. Mrs F's biography is on the company website."

"Why did she drug Georgia Flanders, though?" asked Glenis, who had been listening to the conversation.

"I don't think she did. Georgia got drunk and passed out; there were no drugs in her system," Sarah explained. "She was sad at the loss of her grandmother and wanted her father's attention."

"What an actress that Patty was – she had me fooled," said Charles. "Ruthless killer, I'm pleased she's out of sight along with that miserable Emma."

The evening ended with Prudence delivering the aria *When I am Laid in Earth* by Puccini from the opera *Dido and Aeneas*, during which many tears were shed among the group as they each became lost in thoughts. Rapturous applause filled the ballroom as she took her final curtsy.

"I take it you'll be going home tomorrow?" Rachel asked Deep.

"Yes, I've arranged for my luggage to be removed. I'll fly to Delhi and then get a train home. It's been quite an adventure, but now I miss my family and appreciate them more than ever."

"Let's drink to that," said Glenis.

They all raised their glasses.

"To family," they chimed and clinked glasses.

Rachel and Sarah said goodnight to their new friends with Rachel promising to join them for dinner the next day. Deep hugged her.

"I can't thank you enough, Rachel. You are a wonderful person and I'm sure your father is exceptionally proud of you. I wish you every happiness in your marriage and for your future."

A few tears stung the back of Rachel's eyes as she said goodbye to this gentle man.

The next morning Waverley joined Sarah and Rachel as they were eating breakfast. His jaunty bounce told them all was well.

"I just wanted to tell you some good news before I leave for a proper honeymoon this time," he beamed. "Mrs Chowdry has come out of her coma and is showing remarkable resilience. She doesn't yet remember the day of the attack, but the doctors feel certain that her memory will return over time. The police don't need her to testify as they have enough evidence with the taped confession from yesterday and with her husband no longer providing Patty Chambers with an alibi. Robert Hutchins has been released and he is already on his way home to England."

"Thank you, Chief," said Sarah.

"Goodbye for now, ladies. Remember we always have a job for you, Rachel."

As Waverley strode away, Rachel looked at her friend.

"He never gives up, does he?"

"You love it, Rachel Prince. Now how about we explore what New Zealand has to offer?"

"That I am looking forward to. You're on, Nurse Bradshaw."

THE END

Acknowledgements

Thank you to my editor Alison Jack, as always, for her kind comments about the book and for suggestions, corrections and amendments that make it a more polished read.

Thanks to my beta readers for comments and suggestions, and for their time given to reading the early drafts.

Thanks to my immediate circle of friends who are so patient with me when I'm absorbed in my fictional world and for your continued support in all my endeavours.

I have to say thank you to my cruise loving friends for joining me on some of the most precious experiences of my life and to the cruise lines for making every holiday a special one.

Author's Note

Thank you for reading *Dying to Cruise*, the fourth book in my *Rachel Prince Mystery* series. If you have enjoyed it, please leave an honest review on Amazon and/or any other platform you may use. I love receiving feedback from readers and can assure you that I read every review.

Keep an eye out for Book 5 in the *Rachel Prince Mystery* series. *A Christmas Cruise Murder* is due for release in late autumn 2019.

Keep in touch:
Sign up for my no-spam newsletter at:
https://www.dawnbrookespublishing.com

Follow me on Facebook:
https://www.facebook.com/dawnbrookespublishing/

Follow me on Twitter:
@dawnbrookes1

Follow me on Pinterest:
https://www.pinterest.co.uk/dawnbrookespublishing

About the Author

Dawn Brookes is author of the *Rachel Prince Mystery* series, combining a unique blend of murder, cruising and medicine with a touch of romance.

Dawn has a 39-year nursing pedigree and takes regular cruise holidays, which she says are for research purposes! She brings these passions together with a Christian background and a love of clean crime to her writing.

The surname of her protagonist is in honour of her childhood dog, Prince, who used to put his head on her knee while she lost herself in books.

Bestselling author of *Hurry up Nurse: memoirs of nurse training in the 1970s* and *Hurry up Nurse 2: London calling*, Dawn worked as a hospital nurse, midwife, district nurse and community matron across her career. Before turning her hand to writing for a living, she had multiple articles published in professional journals and co-edited a nursing textbook.

She grew up in Leicester, later moved to London and Berkshire, but now lives in Derbyshire. Dawn holds a Bachelor's degree with Honours and a Master's degree in education. Writing across genres, she also writes for children. Dawn has a passion for nature and loves animals, especially dogs. Animals will continue to feature in her children's books as she believes caring for animals and nature helps children to become kinder human beings.

Other Books by Dawn Brookes

Rachel Prince Mysteries

A Cruise to Murder

Deadly Cruise

Killer Cruise

Dying to Cruise

Memoirs

Hurry up Nurse: memoirs of nurse training in the
1970s

Hurry up Nurse 2: London calling

Hurry up Nurse 3: More adventures in the life of a
student nurse

Coming Soon 2019

Book 5 in the *Rachel Prince Mystery* series

A Christmas Cruise Murder

Look out for New Crime Novel Series in 2020

Murder in Elm Wood

Picture Books for Children

Ava & Oliver's Bonfire Night Adventure
Ava & Oliver's Christmas Nativity Adventure
Danny the Caterpillar
Gerry the One-Eared Cat

.

Printed in Great
Britain
by Amazon